MOON

ON

WATER

Other Works by Matthew Gasda

The American Sublime: Two Poetry Collections

MOON ON WATER

A novel by Matthew Gasda

Serpent Club Press

Serpent Club Press books may be purchased for educational, business, or sales
promotional use. For more information please contact Serpent Club Press at
theserpentclub@gmail.com

Second Edition.
First printed in 2013 by Serpent Club Press.

Interior design by Emily Gasda
Set in Williams Caslon

ISBN
978-0-615-87062-5

LCCN
2013950163

For my friend Keith Smith

M

"But this, its faithlessness, manifests itself also in another way; it becomes simply a repetition."

-Kierkegaard, *Either/Or*

y need to write comes now, a year later. The months have passed quickly and yet, in my memory they are like a paper ocean set on stage: each slowly sawing back and forth, creating a movement not unlike water when seen from a distance.

2

A girl and her brother run through the fountain in Washington Square. The girl is not unaware of her charm—how the water makes her dress cling to her thighs—how she is buried in a moonlight which is like snowflakes (or goose-feathers)—and how she looks like a marble bird diving through the clouds for pearls:

The scene reminds me of something La Rondine once said to me—something that I said I would never forget—but what was it?—that she'd trust me, always, that love requires faith.

And at midnight the fountain shuts off, the water becomes bashful, and the children dip their feet beneath the cool, unrippling surface...

In Paris, that night in August when we met—what did she read to me?—something about a moon on the water...

Later, she wrote to me and said that she would remember me by pressing the glass of me against the mirror of her body. She said her hand engraved a choice, like a Palm Sunday of echoes and stones.

(And by writing this down I may still remember something yet.)

It lapses now, the ashes of roses, La Seine the night I kissed her...something about those metaphysical rivers.

And I woke up early this morning trying to remember who I was with her, and who she was with me—thinking that I'd forgotten what she looked like: the sound of a gypsy accordion painted in blue, or a poem bundled together with a sheaf of flowers.

Tempr' era dal principio mattino:

I fall in love with someone new every day just to feel that sorrow again: the fable of the body praying itself into something other than what it was, and the sense that we're always midway along an infinite path, La Rondine and I—breaking off like fractals inside a paper equation.

Because then, openly, out of the blue, we recognized each other: the gramophone sadness of Paris; La Seine shuffling itself like a deck of cards; the dismantled erotic grammar of just-after-midnight; a muffled accordion begging not to be forgotten.

She mailed me Rilke's *Letters to a Young Poet* and all of a sudden I understood: that La Rondine had a way of speaking to me across oceans of time, and the rivers we never crossed...because she quoted the memoirs of French writers and said that life was a horror, or that: *no*—life was the overture to Mendelssohn's *A Midsummer Night's Dream*...and because she said I was like a Zen archer pointing the wrong way—and because there was hunger, because there were hymns of *Edelweiss* and *Fear no more the heat of the sun*—and because she met me behind Notre Dame, read chapter 20 of *La Rayuela* and told me that that's why she was in Paris—because of that book, that chapter— and because I said the same was true of me, and because it really was.

And it remains undeciphered, even today, what that meant to both of us: that first night, and what happened afterwards, and everything—*everything* that we managed to make happen and everything that didn't: the adagio from Mahler's *9th*, our lungs breathing light, a house all our own, a trip to the sea, torn pajamas, fried eggs, the beautiful stillness of being alone together.

And what we ended up with instead were raindrops that plowed a field in the air, flowers grown from elegies, sent/unsent letters—pleas for understanding passed back and forth like voices in a choir.

La Rondine, Paris, the mirror[1] that gives back all loveliness—all of these enchantments are hidden behind paper screens; a queen in opal, a chessboard mimicking dialects—a meaning we gave up because we were afraid we'd lose it.

---

1 We were like two butterflies pinned (and shivering) together, beating our wings against the air, our hands falling away from each other's faces like secret tears or the dancers in *Café Müller*.

And why do I bother chasing Lena across the fountain in Washington Square?—like I chase La Rondine across time—because we made up a game, inserted that game inside a language, let the game flower like a seed inside a jar.

But Lena makes things up too: that her mother was a dancer in the London Royal Ballet, that her father was born in Central Park like a tree, that she was a gypsy for a year in Alexandria who survived by dancing in the street, that her ancestors included Galileo, Stendhal, Chekhov, Manet, Monet, Matisse, and Godard...

And watch: Lena writes lipstick parables on the walls while she listens to *The Songs of Leonard Cohen.*

Watch: we talk about filling an entire literary magazine with our poems. She says she'll use the *nom de plume* "La Rondine" just to annoy me (she's been reading my notebooks).

And we each read a book by Kafka. She chooses *Letters to Felice.* I choose *Letters to Milena.*[2] Later, she cuts up both books and glues together a third edition from the scraps, calls it *Letters to Filena.* She paints a portrait of me reading *Letters to Filena*—mounts it over the bed—calls it *Kafka's Revenge...*

Lena takes lovers out of boredom, I realize, and insecurity, and because of the physical necessity that all people have for more and more contact.

She lets her lovers finish in her hands, her mouth, on her stomach, in her hair. She likes kissing women when it rains—at least that's what she tells me—

She says that I'm swimming after transcendence like I'm trying to pluck a message back from the waves.

2 I am constantly trying to communicate something incommunicable, to explain something inexplicable, to tell about something I only feel in my bones and which can only be experienced in those bones. Basically it is nothing other than this fear we have so often talked about; a fear spread to everything, fear of the greatest as of the smallest...fear, paralyzing fear of pronouncing a word, although this fear may not only be fear, but also a longing for something greater than all that is fearful.

Notes piling on top of notes like cellular proteins: shape, complexity emerging out of chaos—the cornet was one of those gorgeous accidents that nobody could explain.

"To call the *St. Louis Blues* an accident would be to confuse an accident with a miracle," M said, leaning over to Jove, who was smoking next to him on the floor.

Go Satchmo, go!

Belmonte sat down on the futon, lit a cigarette, and vanquished his third or fourth Irish coffee of the night with considerable disdain for everything.

"The overture is a series of trials before the final test, which is the opera itself...we kill what we love, et cetera, et cetera..." Belmonte lectured. "True tragic sorrow requires guilt—of course—requires the pain of innocence, the element of transparency...the total opaqueness of the spirit..."

"And very, very, very slowly," M thought, "we might find our way toward a little bit of living impulse in the blues—in this wave of dialectics—a sound; a sine—a metaphysical song..."

"The Bergsonian universe—the universe of time, obviously—" Belmonte continued, "pops like a cloud, and there, one can find a complete breakdown of form—a choral mass. A string quartet broken into pieces...in the concept of space/time, then, you've got an absolutely new concept of what reality might be—a four dimensional dance, no different than a modern novel. A relativity poem."

It was raining heavily outside. Cadence, stress, tonality: strings of energy weaving and shuttling together in the predawn half-darkness.

"Do either of you ever feel incomprehensibly knotted up with words?—" M asked suddenly, "because it's killing me."

Belmonte rubbed his cigarette out on the floor and shrugged.

"Only through dialectics can...some kind of higher consciousness...Orestes the Impure, you know..."

M frowned.

Belmonte gestured with a flame-tipped hand.

"I'm saying that the world died when salvation became more important than sex...when power became everything between people—but fuck it M—why are you getting so serious about this anyway?"

"Out of ourselves we compose a book of disquietude," Jove said mystically, suddenly, slowly.

"You know, according to an unconfirmed anecdote, Saint-Saëns stormed out of the première of *Le sacre du printemps*— infuriated over what he considered the misuse of the bassoon," Belmonte added.

It was getting late.

(Everyone was beginning to take nonsense for granted.)

Schubert songs and ruby dresses...

Futures we didn't believe in.

"Remember me when I've gone away."

(A battered rendition of Catullus—probably drunk.)

We were more idiotic than we needed to be when we were together—but then again, we were inspired. We were inspired because we were full of shit, and because we were always trying to get each other into bed, and because we were always seeing other people while the other wasn't looking, and because we both liked things that way, and because we didn't.

And yes, that was the beautiful part—that we had this *either/or* in front of us the whole time: an *either/or* that underwrote our whole affair.

This was the modern art show of sex without orgasm; orgasm without love—

Her paintings were full of pagan images, strange geometries—the ashes that were always sweeping across New York City...Joni Mitchell blues...wings clipped with fire.

And we would talk about poets every night until we'd fall asleep—Gauguin was a poet, Pissarro was a dauber.

Stevens was a painter, Eliot was a dauber. Char, Rimbaud, Stravinsky, Joyce, Proust, Debussy, Malick, Kandinsky, Mahler, Chekhov, Schubert, Ozu, Bolaño, Musil, Delacroix: all poets.

Foster Wallace, Picasso, Mondrian, Hemingway, Kerouac, Ginsberg, Miles Davis, Auden, George Eliot, Mozart, Renoir: all daubers.

(Though I disagreed about Renoir and somewhat about Mozart.)

We both agreed that our lists, really, could be extended *ad infinitum*—and to no one's benefit—and that the lists didn't make sense, anyway, because they were so inconsistent and so unfair...

Once Lena tried to teach Jove how to draw the male body. She also tried to teach him Spanish and Portuguese. She also tried to set him up on dates with her painter friends.

Jove said he wanted beauty, not brains.

(The results, of course, were indescribable.)

It was more romantic to throw stones and be casual about everything—to listen to records that made both of them cry and not say anything about it—than to actually say *something* and consequently admit that the world had wounded both of them.

They believed in unplucked apples, loves just out of reach, paradoxes about paradox, desires for desire.

They played Chopin's *Nocturne in C* on his record player until New York became their city and no one else's—until everything around them sunk like a flower-petal in a clear pool.

They didn't want to listen to anyone else; they didn't want advice—they didn't need any: they had Chopin and his nocturnes; they had spring mornings cold enough to wake them up without an alarm; they had novels yet-to-be-read; poems always on the verge of being written into stone.

And M said that his poems would mimic her paintings—that he would use blue shades until his words resembled a moon on water: until he remembered what he was writing about, and who he was writing for.

Lena said that his poems were like roses that had been choked by two strong hands; roses that had turned blue—roses that had been held under water. (Roses gasping for air.)

They fucked in taxis that they couldn't pay for. They fucked because they wanted to; because they liked doing it in cabs—and because they liked running from the bill.

Lena asked him sometimes what he was thinking about—but she always knew how he would answer: *eleatically*.

(None of these were things that he told Joanna about in his letters.)

Everything on the level of experience was fused together like the tones of a piano sonata for four hands: garbage and flowers, winter and summer, Kafka and Ingres, midday and midnight, Lena and La Rondine...Jove and Belmonte unspooling metaphysical yarn on the floor, Wallace and Ellebelle arguing in their room, Herzen and his poems, recited halfway down the hall...

"Mahler feared writing his tenth symphony."

"Of course he did—because Beethoven croaked trying to write his...and superstitions aside, you have to admit M, that—"

"Hey, have any of you ever seen the Visconti version of *Death in Venice?*" Ellebelle asked, coyly entering the living room in one of Wallace's oversized t-shirts.

"Yes," M said.

"No," Jove and Belmonte said.

"In theory," Herzen said.

"He uses Mahler extensively throughout the film—" Ellebelle explained, "that's why I mentioned it."

"Elle, come back to bed—" Wallace called weakly from the bedroom.

"The use of the adagio in the fifth—" M said softly, "music like opening your eyes in the dark..."

Pretty and *ultra-Parisian* Ellebelle sat in the open bedroom window and smoked wistfully. Time *was* something absolutely golden, just like consciousness—and the two things were mutually transforming right there before her eyes.

The transformation was what was great about nights in Brooklyn like this—though Wallace would probably wake up in a second, wanting to have sex again, because that's just how Saturday nights went for them; because that's what anyone would have expected from two artists sleeping together in Brooklyn, and because that was what they expected from themselves: restless attempts at union, aborted attempts at getting the other's attention.

You were supposed to lay around, anyway, Ellebelle thought, watching time and consciousness play like cats with a ball of thread on the floor; and that's what she was doing—even though she wished she had just been able to fall asleep like Wallace, with a sweet, dreamless thud.

Earlier that night, after they had eaten dinner and retreated to their bedroom, Wallace had started by peeling off her sweater, while she began by dropping her skirt to her ankles so that he could then peel off her underwear and apply his mouth to her cunt; a move which, while not surprising, had knocked her against the wall, so that she had moaned slightly, turning her head towards the ceiling with a smile.

It had felt, at that moment, like a million years since he had been inside of her, pleasing her with his tongue, making her feel like a woman and not just a doll. She had started to cum, and when she did, he came up and dried his mouth on her collarbone, and kissed her on the neck, and then the mouth...

But did she really love him?—that was all she could think about for the rest of the night—or was this just the way that she coped with life?—letting him please her in his predictable, dogged sort of way— and he *did* please her—incredibly, awfully, arbitrarily—she realized.

They moved each other because they had chosen each other, and not other people: because it was each other's spit and cum that they sucked down on short nights after long days of work, because they drank their beers slowly to get through hot summer afternoons indoors...and because they fucked in the shower to get ready for work, or to take the edge off in the evenings, or just to cool down a little when the sidewalks really started baking in July...and because they had been together for so long, that they had forgotten what it would be like, *really*, to be with anyone else.

Life was endless ribbons, flowers, artificial fruits; life was the finery of emptiness which some still-life painter would copy down one day after they got married or broke up—or both; one right after the other...

She wanted to grovel at his feet, she wanted him to flip her over on her stomach and fuck her so hard that she cried. Loving someone meant surrendering your will: it meant *destroying it*. Loving someone should be like loving a god, she thought, that was the most obvious thing in the world to everyone but Wallace...

And Ellebelle was wholly human before she even knew herself; she was so human that she didn't know what to do with Saturday nights, with coffee like a Greek tragedy, with the fragrance of late May right on the cusp of June. It was pain that was indifferent to the sky she realized, looking through the bedroom door at M, who was writing[3] something in his journal, and then back at Wallace, who was fast asleep in their bed.

3 Sometimes I have the feeling that we're in one room with two opposite doors and each of us holds the handle of one door, one of us flicks an eyelash and the other is already behind his door, and now the first one has but to utter a word and immediately the second one has closed his door behind him and can no longer be seen. He's sure to open the door again for it's a room which perhaps one cannot leave. If only the first one were not precisely like the second, if he were calm, if he would only pretend not to look at the other, if he slowly set the room in order as though it were a room like any other; but instead he does exactly the same as the other at his door, sometimes even both are behind the doors and the beautiful room is empty.

She could suffer because she had become an adult or she could lay down and die: those were her only two options, unless there were others, and she thought that maybe there were others, only she hadn't discovered them yet—

And because I should have known that I would begin to look for La Rondine everywhere: in the margins of novels, floating in a beer glass at Roberta's, in pool halls and bookstores and coffee shops...in the grooves of old records, and in the wasted landscape of the Far Rockaways after the hurricane swept everything into the sea like crushed cans swept into a plastic bag.

And because like Jove says—the river of time carries us on like silt into the Nile delta; and because we're looking for a way to swim back upstream; and because we're all whores for a purity which we will never attain...

And when Lena couldn't stop crying in Port Authority, I came to understand that I'd arranged my life too abstractly for any real sincerity to trickle down and seep into my affairs, and that—like any hypocrite who moves to Brooklyn to write poetry—I was too caught up in *RE-MEM-BER-ING* than actually *LIV-ING*, as Jove would put it if I said all this to him.

Paris had blushed with annihilation, *sure*—La Rondine and I could have burrowed inside of time right then and there, like larvae, and waited to hatch into a dreamlike eternity, so that I wouldn't have to look through my life, like I do now, with Proustian binoculars—but we didn't—and so I do.

And so La Rondine comes into focus like my own personal Odette and rouses the death in me, gives it a cup of gin, so that, it—the death in me—smiles, and lets her sing it to sleep.

But then again, tracing the blue surface of old records, and tasting the thunder and the damp of the apartment, and the two-week-old laundry, and Jove's cigarettes, and Ellebelle's cigarettes, and Wallace's canned olives, and Belmonte's cigarettes, and everybody's morning-old coffee in the sink—tasting and internalizing and phenomenologizing all these things—I realize that *this* is the only way to live: with one foot squarely in the empyrium of the romantic past, and one foot squarely in the sensual empyrium of the unromantic present, and one foot obtusely in the existentially terrifying empyrium of the distant and semi-romantic future...

And it's also my belief that people will need religion until we reach a point of mathematical unlimitedness (when negation becomes absolute)—and because nothing seems, at least to me, to equate to the transcendental, except what I know as myself, and what everyone else knows as the circumference of meaning—which is poetry.

And around here, the streets are always disappearing around the corner, nights soak themselves in the brine of darkness, and the white leaves of torn up letters cross themselves in space as they fall from the canopy of sky.

And after long silences I tend to let myself become horrified by my own reflective innocence—at least that's what Jove says, and I think he's right.

A phrase, a disjunction: these things bring us forward in time only so that we have the vantage of futurity rather than belatedness.

Merde.[4]

4 And when that mold of consciousness is broken, and its liquid dross pours out—who is responsible for cleaning up that pool of shining, half-molten gold? Who recreates the happiness of certain, random, unspoken moments between people? Who puts these arabesques into forms and calls them poems? Is it Jove—with his spiritual art, his adherence to the stage of Stanislavski, which is the theater of life? And what does it mean to feel everything and say nothing? To see that differences between people are sustained only by selfish, almost hysterical illusions? "Look how you move through the world," Jove says to me. "Ripples, ripples and ripples...they rippled over the river, rippling..." The River Of Time—is it separate from fate?—the three women with ravaged faces? no—we're discussing the same thing. The old women. Fate. "The River Of Time flowing through all things." The mold of consciousness, like jelly in a tin, dropped to the floor...the overhead light in the living room stops working. Ellebelle takes out black and white photographs from when she was in college, talks about them wistfully; the glory days of art school. Belmonte talks about the twilight of the west; the island of Ikaria where old Greek men never die...twilight everywhere, passionate and simple. Wallace plays guitar, in his room, badly, with the door open. Someone turns up the record, which is Leonard Cohen's *Songs from a Room*.

An Orpheus picks swanhood, an Ajax a lion, but an Odysseus wants the quiet life[5] of a man.

La Rondine had told me that people were ancient storms that had become stuck like glue in the trees—and that was La Rondine's great secret—that she could see all the invisible parts of nature—that she knew that making love was dangerous and therefore to be avoided except in moments of absolute surrender...that love meant vertigo: that it meant snatching at handfuls of melting clouds.

La Rondine and I resembled Aristophanes' theory of lovers, in other words—we were like a knucklebone cut in two.

And she could read ancient Greek—she started reciting The Iliad to me once in a Milanese bookstore—where I'd found her the summer after Paris—which made me feel like Keats looking into Chapman's Homer.

And I remember the dark earliness of her body; the ramification of her whispering in my ear; her blood rising like water through a broken flower-stem.

And this is all so incredibly vague because all I have to remember her by is a single photograph taken in a metro station photobooth with "*10-13 Giugno 2011*" written in black ink on the back—and because I've needed to forget necessary things about her in order to take one non-Eleatic step through the world (New York), lest I take none.

(And the only orientation,[6] the only stance towards time and remembering that matters, is the awareness that time can not be made to stand still: that time is that matrix which supports the whole flux of material above it.)

5 There is nothing like a second death before the first, but a conversation between strangers inevitably involves third, fourth, fifth, and sometimes even sixth deaths, in rapid succession.

6 Each of us has his own way of emerging from the underworld, mine is by writing. That's why the only way I can keep going, if at all, is by writing: not through rest and sleep. I am far more likely to achieve peace of mind through writing than I am likely to achieve the capacity to write through peace.

And the answer is yes: I'm haunted by time, as much as I'm haunted by anything, and as much as anything haunts anyone else—but I'm comfortable enough with time to enjoy it too; comfortable with the way it haunts me and with the way it makes me uncomfortable and sad when I'm doing simple things like riding the subway, or ordering a cup of coffee, or laying on my roof in the morning and watching the clouds peel the moon away like the rind from a blood orange.

And it would be morally preferable, I'm sure, to dissolve any unity that begins to emerge from the disparate elements of my life, but it's against my instincts to do that (to strain away the whey of one's whole self)—because even if my becoming a unified, clarified human being would be obnoxious and painful to others (which it would), I wouldn't mind, because simply, I would be happy.

And my instincts are also to cling to the past; to try to resuscitate moments that lack for oxygen—and isn't that what writing's for?—and all idealism too?—the separating of the past from the present; the untangling of Aphrodite from the bed of Mars...

Mental pictures get filed into albums and stored away—and they're damn annoying to dig up again, and the all colors fade, except for the yellows (and only the really bright yellows too).

And I tell myself I don't need it anymore (remembering)—and maybe I really don't—but I'm surrounded by a conspiracy of silence, and that just makes me nervous as hell.

When I moved to New York I figured I would escape from time, and therefore the past, but that's not what's happened at all:

I still wake up experiencing the perilous vertigo of wanting more from my own being than my poor being can give...

And what I experience now is the charm of living inside a tiny cluster—of being an inkblot on a page of the mind—an inkblot as complex as DNA, or Joyce, or one of Joanna's letters—because the otherness and strangeness of life is too absolute to deny it—the textuality of being alive—and like Jove always tells me: the pain of human beings is too magnificent to indicate that we are anything other than cosmic playthings, and that for this reason, people are the most significant things in the universe, and the least significant at the same time.

Jove imagined that people floated down the river of time, and that he was the only human being who was allowed to stand on the shore and not float away: that it was his responsibility to set the little paper boats of the soul down in the water and see them off into infinity. It was an absurd and grandiose image: boat after boat, folded in his hands, set off onto the stream of forever.

"Why am I always on the outside of time, and no one else?" Jove thought. "Why am I always the one running out into storms, crying out for lightning to hit me?"

Belmonte imagined that M, Jove, and everyone else were floating in a pond, rather than the river of time—where he, Belmonte, was an angler, sitting lazily by the water, with his pants rolled up to his knees. The fish that he caught in the pond he threw back, or gutted for lunch. It was better, Belmonte believed, to be gutted, than to be thrown back.

M considered the Nile to be the most metaphysical river of rivers, not only because it was upside down, but because it divided the living from the dead. Everyone, he knew, was a phantom on one side of the river, or the other.

"In the dream I had last night, I was a giant laying on a white beach," Jove rehearsed. "The sun was so bright that I couldn't open my eyes and all I could hear was the water rushing around me...and the sound was fucking HUGE, like an ocean that had wrapped itself around the whole fucking world...or just my head...and sometimes I dream I'm an angel, but instead of feathers, I have two eyes in my back—where the wings would be—and instead of flying, I just see EVERYTHING in the WORLD..."

"Angels—" Belmonte interrupted, very dryly, "are a

symbol[7] of God's desire to populate His heaven with creatures who amuse Him."

"DAMN—"

"Now let me tell you a joke..." Belmonte paused to pour more gin into his coffee. "A man wakes up to his alarm clock in Hell and asks the devil what time it is. *Eternity,* the devil says."

7   M thought he had a thousand symbols to represent La Rondine (but they were all either too particular or too abstract): the lunch she had for him the first afternoon in Milan (barley, peas, carrots), her voice (elastic, liquid), her touch (pagan, Catholic), her Catholicism (philosophical, Italian), her Italian (melancholy, liquid), her paganism (Catholic, sensual), her Milanese (northern, Italian), her modernity (sensual, Catholic), her movements (Milanese, philosophical), her silences (pagan, Italian), her philosophy (sensual, pagan, Catholic, Milanese, Italian) and so on.

And I was bitter when I began. Bitter writing the novel. Bitter writing the film. Bitter ash. Bitter oleander. Bitter when I was in love. Bitter when I was out of love. Bitter when I started again. Bitter because I haven't stopped.

And bitter because I haven't lived up to the promise of the love I felt.

And bitter because love doesn't work out in practice—only in Romantic theory.[8]

And because bitterness took root and became bitter; because I let bitterness flower...

And it would take a virtuoso act of the imagination to bring the lyrical and the tragic together, like in Chekhov (master of bitterness, author of *The Three Sisters*)—and I'm just looking for some real, individual expression around here to correspond to the bittersweet happiness (the word is *glukupikron* in the Greek) of desire...

"And better to go dignified old man," I'm thinking, "into the void of routine, than to try to wring the bitterness out of the day-old, month-old, year-old tea-leaves I've tried to tell the future by..."

Or no—better to live and have *togetherness:*

Hart Crane's letters, Hart Crane's poems, the relentless frenzy of self with universe, the stars imposing themselves on Washington Square, Dante's lyrical flowers all-white wayside blue, Jove writing in his dream journal, Jove crying about another beautiful boy who broke his heart, Jove telling me about Zen

8   "Signal a character out of solitude. Bring her over and ask her to change your life."

eroticism, and about being true rather than false[9]...Lena reading *Young Werther* in German and telling me that this was a book written for me, and me laughing and saying don't be ridiculous...

And Lena reading upside down in bed. And Lena crying because I'm taking the bus out of New York from Port Authority...

"Die early to avoid fate..."

(This is what we tell ourselves.)

Memory atones for later disregard. Memory takes the place of fate in our tragedy of hands, faces, paper-kites...

(Swann pulls up Odette's dress—pushes her face first onto the bed.)

---

9   True to anything, true to love, true to prayer, true to death, true to friendship, true to sex, true to literature, true to theater, true to prayer, true even to bullshit.

A mint plant, a basil—a burst of seeds climbing up the windowsill; Lena talking to me from the bath—

"How terrible dying is M…"

"Can I put on a late quartet please?—the fourteenth…all the sadness of the world…"

"Close the door, I'm cold!"

And the white-flowered jasmine—something we only dream about—having a place in the country, not having computers, burying our phones in the ground, marking the seasons by changes in the wind and stars…painting with our hands, writing poems on paper-plates and greeting cards…waking up as early or as late as we like.

"The music is so sad, can you turn it up?"

"…"

"Watch the clouds of steam from the hot water…they're like dreams…and can you get my dress please it's hanging up on the door—thank you dearest—thank you—"

Echo's bones. A body annulled by nakedness. A jar of moonshine open on the counter.[10]

"M *do you hear it?*—Beethoven knew he was dying—can you believe it?—writing music like that with your last gasp?—the terror—"[11]

---

10 Confessions pour in and out of the mind like water through a water-clock. Each moment goes in no particular direction. We count it against ourselves in the general scheme of our moral existence.

11 "Only people who are capable of loving strongly can also suffer great sorrow, but this same necessity of loving serves to counteract their grief and heals them," M read aloud. "What is that from?" Lena asked curiously. "I think it's taken from a letter written by God to the universe," M said. "Oh, so you're reading Tolstoy," Lena said, yawning, trying not to fall asleep in the tub. "Yes, that's it exactly," M said.

16

A woman in patent leather boots and man in a maroon raincoat meet on the corner of 11th and A and get into a taxi.

A single leaf detaches itself from a tree at the end of the street, and floats at a speed which allows it to strike the windshield of the taxi, momentarily, before being swept into oblivion.

The woman in patent leather boots refuses to accept that the moment around her is still, elegant, pliant. The young man in the maroon raincoat watches the flow of pedestrian traffic mold itself around the car like a glove: people immersed in their phones, radically busy, unable to look up at the two people watching them from the taxi.

The taxi-driver is a Prospero figure, staying an illusion that will lead to marriage: that taxi leads them to the place they have always expected to go.

(There is an indefinite expansion of an interval of time, of the mental space they both inhabit.)

The woman in patent leather boots puts her head on the shoulder of the young man in the maroon raincoat. The young man in the maroon raincoat takes out a novel from under his arm. The woman in patent leather boots asks him what he's reading.

He says something about silence and permanent incommunicability.

She asks him what he means.

He doesn't answer.

Everything gets filtered through the pores of life. Until there is nothing left. Until there is nothing left, but what can't be washed or blown away in the rain.

(Grief falls like raindrops from the sky.)

Death, love, childhood, self-deception, isolation, purpose— the desire to communicate doesn't dissipate, but instead, it ends up revealing the impossibility of most forms of truthful expression.

(What we know by heart can never be lost, in other words.)

Skim back: I accuse La Rondine of being scared—but what am I really trying to say?—she accuses me of not listening to her, and she is right; we are both right in parallel ways.

Skim ahead: we are never sure of our sorrow. Dead years draw us together. We need more than intimacy: we need shared consciousness, shared ideograms, shared disclosures. We want to immerse ourselves in the hair-raising strangeness of anything, *anything*—other than ourselves...

Skim ahead: consciousness is what we pour into a translucent mold; the mold hardens until it resembles an impersonal address to the sky.

Remember: youth is akin to rain: rain is akin to spiritual cleanliness.

Remember: the chestnut trees around here are immense— in my dreams they tower over the city blocks like giants from a forgotten (or discarded) mythology.

Remember: thunder—*that darkening*—is a celebration of associative chaos: the kind that people perceive as hiding just below the seemingly calm surface of the earth (which itself is already embedded in a swinging, pendant-galaxy).

Skim ahead: I'm trying to re-compass a mode of being—a violent transparence.

Stay where you are: a few things that I don't want to forget so easily (Bach, Scarlatti, Beethoven's 9th, some early quartets,

Stravinsky, Prokofiev, Monteverdi's *Orfeo,* Bix on the cornet, Keats' letters, Lena, La Rondine. Something about the Jardin des Plantes. Joanna and the wonderful deafness of her writing; a dark piano thrown down the stairs)...

Through tunnels of pain we advance.

Through tunnels of pain we retreat.

Go back to the beginning: La Rondine is like Debussy's *Quartet in G.* I love the paradox of her voice, I love the way she moves her hands when she speaks, the way she kisses me, and the way she is sensitive to everything I say, and everything I don't.

And because of her, through a not-so-final tunnel of pain I retreat.[12]

12 She moves through Milan like she is discovering someone's private Japanese garden; seeking out every particle of light, sound, and color; seeking the angels who live to throw stones from the tops of the trees. She tells me about the butterflies she seals in mason jars; butterflies that never die. She says that we can't make love because I will be gone by the morning—she says it will destroy her. (She says that we met in a previous life.)

Lena met M a month after he had returned from Milan.

He read his poems to her. They danced in Prospect Park. They made love every night for a year. He never said anything about La Rondine. He never said anything to her about his other affairs; he mainly talked about books—

He said he was making a film called Three Days In Milan[13]—but he never said what it was about.

He went to secretive meetings of the literati—and often said he was busy revising the script for his film. She told him she loved him. He didn't say he loved her at first—but eventually he would admit that he did, that he loved her.

They made each other angry. He would become angry with Lena in a way that he never would with anyone else. It had to do with the way she pouted whenever he had to leave—whenever he wanted to draw a circle[14] for himself that didn't include her within its circumference.

And it was above all because she resisted knowing about the lovers who populated his heart like huge crowds of bourgeoisie spilling out of an old Parisian arcade; because she only admitted of a reality in which she was his sole lover, and because she clung to her belief like it was a life raft afloat on a vast, Pascalian silence.

Lena wanted him to yield to the strength of her emotions— he thought this was childish—and so they fought endlessly.

"Love is life to me. All, everything that I understand, I understand only because I love. Everything is, everything exists, only because I love. Everything is united by it alone. Love is God, and to die means that I, a particle of love, will return to the general and eternal source," Lena told him once.

13 In Milan, there is a sense that one waits at the door to all of Italy, that one is an old, charmed flâneur, attached to the memory of loveliness, while, in Grand Central, poised to enter New York, one feels, for a moment, at least, that one has slipped out of the strictures of time; that one could be, if one only closed one's eyes, in a different time: 1950 or 1925 or 1905.
14 His letters to Joanna went in circles, too. Everything did.

Spring begins when she opens the door, and spring ends when she leaves in her typical flourish (in her beautiful darkness on the verge of light).

And each separate petal of her is a negation at the same time it is an affirmation: a return to first and last things (day and night, love and death). And we ask ourselves what the earth has suffered, and whether we can retrieve its glory in a glance, or in the joining of our hands. And we draw a luminous outline around New York City: we overwhelm ourselves with distance before drawing close again; we overwhelm ourselves with the fragrance of invisible flowers, oil paints, and coffee grounds. And we agree that leaving each other would be a mercy like no other; we agree that it would be better to be alone—but inwardly, we know that we are already joined in a way that will not suffer to be broken.

And we have a way of speaking to each other that avoids the prismatic silence of anger and disappointment: we scatter our serenity, we transform sex into a pure, almost listless gesture.

(We push our mouths into one jell, we adjust the curtains, we give our full consent, our full and joyous consent, to the dreadfulness of life...near-disintegration, love, a   continual conversion of the visible.)

Afterwards, he always went home thinking that maybe he missed *it* with Alice, what *it* was.

It never mattered what they talked about—or where they met: there was always a choir singing between them, lovely as hell, begging the heart to burst open or shred itself to pieces.

M was convinced that there was something unnaturally opaque about the texture of his life, that if he pressed down on it with his hands he'd sink into it forever—but the truth was that he couldn't lessen his own metaphysical burden any more than he could lessen that burden for people he loved.

What he wanted to know was: how could anyone describe the *real* junk?—the loneliness, the *das-ding*, the erotic desire that wakes a person up in the middle of the night?

"Nobody knows what it's *about* anymore—" M thought, "no one ever did and no one ever will know...how to be the loving guardian of another's solitude...how to live in a place where light spreads like a shadow over a mirror...how to suffer longing without turning away...how to suffer the dazzling peristalsis of the throat as emotion passes through it."

"It's the illness of love, really, that staggers me when I'm walking down the street, like I'm sick to my stomach, or knee-deep in lilies—it's really pathetic, I know, but I can't help it, as much as I want to."

He decided that he would walk through Washington Square on his way up to 14th Street—he estimated that he had about an hour before it started to rain.

"You're really like everyone else in New York, old man, except that you're convinced that the purpose of life is to build a kind of Greco-Keatsian urn and throw it off the Brooklyn Bridge in a grandiose gesture to your favorite American poets—which means that most of the time you're not only full of shit (talking to yourself, like you are now)—but that you're guaranteed to become dissatisfied by the ugliness and asymmetry of everything around you...and you're a real sap—you know that?—a real Lear in the storm—"

Raindrops tossed in the wind like grains of rice:

"But then again, given that all hell is about to break loose, maybe what you've got here is a fake dilemma: a consolation disguised as what will certainly be damp socks, damp hair, damp books, damp hair: one of those cleansing, intoxicating, charming *premières* that Olympus puts on stage during the spring season to entertain us wimpy, over-intellectualized mortals—"

"And I actually hope Lena is waiting for me when I get home, and that Wallace hasn't used all the hot water already...and you know what?—each of these raindrops is a miracle, so impossible by itself, yet possible through unity...and look at that woman in the yellow dress running to find shelter in a cafe—I should go and talk to her—pretend that we met before: on the train, or inside a book—"

Life is a joy, even the sad parts, at least that's what it feels like with Neil Young on the record player, and the humidity emptied out by the rain, and Wallace playing guitar in the other room...and hot water for tea on the stove, thank God...

And somehow, taped to my door, there's a little Zen koan[15] written to cure me of my desire for transcendence...

(And it's like *After the Goldrush* released in a swarm—being cured of that desire—being back in the apartment—letting myself sink through the futon like a stone—it's a *pneuma*—a kind of death released from the lungs...a huge welter of activity, a welter of loving, screwing, biting, kicking, scratching, building, tearing down...a lefthook of beauty like an arctic flower...an infant screaming on the subway, a party ending after dawn, a letter arriving three weeks late...)

And still: we treat the apartment like a postscript amended to reality: Wallace's shitty day job, Belmonte's secrets, Jove's acting career, Ellebelle's handmade sweaters, my writing—we all keep our eyes on the sidewalk while we walk, looking for lost pennies and stray sentences.[16]

And what is there to do with this-or-that luminous evening?—with a city-block that opens itself in a congenial disclosure of its impressionistic vistas?

I keep my poems in a funeral urn under my bed. I write them (three or four a day) and roll them up like banknotes and drop

15 *Dear (Stupid) M: Cut a few strands of sunlight like hair and lay those unforgiven strands across the earth. Prayer requires only a voice to court the air with silence, a gash in the tongue to allow for acquisitive vision. You wouldn't eat the honey slathered all over the black bread. You wouldn't whisper even a single Apollonian phrase to me. You will paint your teeth with moonlight. Lena. P.S. I stopped by, but you weren't home, so I talked to Belmonte. He's crazy, isn't he? But he was nice to me, and he isn't nice to anyone.*

16 No one tells us what we're supposed to do here—convictions, obsessions, eccentricities—all this we have to borrow from novels and films. The glory of dissolution is enlarged, it becomes Manhattan, which swallows Brooklyn whole.

them in. I write poems to place myself resolutely in my own time: New York sometime after it became safe and expensive and yuppified. New York long after all the poets joined their first guitar bands. New York like a word processor correction of a typewritten letter. New York like a shout in the street. (History, that is.) And I write poems about courage I'll never have. Poems about sex like a physical wound. Poems like glass sentences dropped on the floor.

And poems are ways of giving and being free. Of looking like Ophelia weighted down by circlets of daisies and buttercups, or Rilke pretending that nothing unusual has happened as a cathedral vaults high before falling into shadow...

And what am I trying to describe?—a breathing-space carved out of a dense wall of carbon dioxide? a mental telescope through which to see the frozen, but still celestial moon?

"*Grief—*" someone whispers in response to something nobody said.

"Look! the light coming in from under the door—"

"Someone is in the hallway—"

"Listen to the rain outside—"

"Lena was here earlier," Ellebelle says to M when he comes in, soaked to the bone.

M talks about the scale of time—the sense of the past—the error of any lie that confines itself to truth—a great ring of eternity eclipsing the Manhattan skyline in a wave of light.

Jove says that M looks like he is moving backwards: absorbing all to himself and to the Brahms that Herzen put on the record player.

Herzen gets M a towel from the bathroom to dry off with.

M says that the music is too painful to listen to—that he should probably go to bed anyway, even though he knows that he won't fall asleep—

M talks about an old man reading Rilke in Washington Square; he talks about seeing through time like through the surface of clear pool; he talks about not giving up on the beauty in himself—*about how no one should give up on the beauty in themselves, no one.*

M goes to his room to change. He throws his wet clothes into a pile against the wall. He can hear Brahms[17] through the door.

Gold and fire. Fruit and leaf.

The rain stops again: a cool wind rushes through the window.

He needs something with *quiddity:* something that he can hold in the palm of his hand like floating candle.

---

17 He wishes someone would turn it off—because the music is so controlled, and because what is being controlled is suffering, and because tragic nobility is the saddest thing in the world.

People with absolute fecundity—people who are charming and beautiful wherever they are and in whatever state of dress or undress— are dangerous and they (You[18]) know it; but without carelessly beautiful people, we wouldn't have poems, or poets for that matter—and the poet in me is grateful, therefore, to have been moderately heartbroken by you.

Plus, I like making the same mistake twice. (I think that's Hericlitus.)

And how does a story change except through gain and loss?

How could I gain you so quickly only to lose you?—

So the story shifts, so I am reconfigured again as soon as I was configured by love. . .

Because I cannot remember you except through the objects I have imagined to take your place.

And because I have always felt that life is the process of recovering something we have never had: the smell of flowers, the rippling of your flank under my hands in the morning. . .

And because I would be unconfined, to spread out across the the city like quicksilver. (No laws and no past, just a fullness and a shapelessness that tries to mimic air—so as to envelope you without having to embrace you with separate arms.)

And because I am not used to this passing of years, where change no longer outpaces love.

18 A few further observations for you, La Rondine, in sequence: 1. You are like the radius of a circle which revenges its beginning by starting over. 2. Miracles are never lies they are only miracles. 3. Events occur because we willed them to occur, but also because they were going to happen no matter what. 4. These are lies, but "so be it" we say: "War, death, famine will happen whether we idealize them or not." 5. You must give your longing a wound and never let it heal.

In between people who are friends but still close to strangers lay the concept of life: *organism, function, order*[19] *of nature: fucking, breathing, music.*

The problem with M, Jove, Wallace and Ellebelle sharing an apartment together was that the financial necessity wasn't worth the interfusion of erotic lives: the inexpressible sense that someone had just fucked that night a few feet from where you were trying to go to sleep—that their spit and semen and vaginal fluid was still drying on the floors, and walls, and blankets; that the process of emotional degradation was still ongoing and increasingly complex, all while you were trying to make dinner, or just write a letter, or watch TV.[20]

"It should be possible," M said to Jove, "to turn yourself into a creature from an imagined world, or learn how to dream while standing up."

"Here is an orphaned idea..." Jove said, staring at the ceiling. "That people are meant to efface themselves before the possibility of self-contradiction."

"I just want to crush as many pulses into the living moment as possible—" M said, "but that's proving extremely difficult."

"The sphere of the moment is drawn around us like a fucking NET—" Jove gesticulated, "but the question is, M, *can you fly by that net?—*"

Jove and M could hear Wallace and Ellebelle fucking through their bedroom door; apparently not without some technical difficulty.

19 It seemed that life ultimately conformed to the same pattern: death, lamentation, birth: friends, family, lovers coming into existence and zooming right on out of it, dividing themselves along the lines of elect and unelect, dreamers and effervescent bourgeoisie.

20 Ellebelle and Wallace poured out the milk curdling in their hands: plastic playthings, paper-plates, the glass shards of their erotic life...people were perfectly beautiful if you were perfectly ignorant of them: indie records from the early nineties, a copy of *Franny and Zooey*, dishes in the sink, socks from winter still on the radiator, the window covered with tape from the hurricane, the tattered Persian rug thankfully vacuumed, the wine bottles lined up against the walls.

"Poor Wallace and poor Ellebelle—" M thought,[21] "certain to be sucked one day back into the whiteish womb of the void, with vast tracts of time and space all around them while they make bad art collages and order Chinese food, and fight, and make love as if they could ward off cosmic disaster with a steady routine of dissatisfaction..."

And he couldn't say he wasn't a part of this, could he?—sitting there at his typewriter, talking to Jove, enjoying a Bossa Nova record and a cup of chamomile tea so much that he could cry, pretending to read a book[22] by Georg Calendula[23] while really having nothing on his mind except the last of the rainwater trembling outside the window.

21 And M could talk about poetry until three in the morning because he never got drunk and because he never stopped believing that you could love somebody through words: and because of this, his presence in the room filled Wallace and Ellebelle with so much nausea and metaphysical sickness, that they had to fuck for three hours with their eyes closed just to cure themselves and forget that he was there.

22 That spring M read *After Babel* (Steiner), *The Professor of Desire* (Roth), *The Alexandria Quartet* (Durrell), *The Brown Book* (Wittgenstein), *What is Metaphysics?* (Heidegger), *Heidegger* (Steiner), *The Endless Rose* (Reiter), *JR* (Gaddis), *Henry James* (Edel), *The Ambassadors* (James), *Duino Elegies* (Rilke), *Tender is the Night* (F.S. Fitzgerald), *The Blue Flower* (P. Fitzgerald) *The Death of Virgil* (Broch), *Journal of Eugene Delacroix* (Eugene Delacroix), *3 Poems* (Ashbery), *Erotic Zen* (Calendula), *This Time* (J. Wallace), *The Selected Letters of Samuel Beckett 1929-1940* (The Selected Samuel Beckett).

23 M's favorite books by Georg Calendula were: *Kant's Theater*, *Van Gogh and Descartes: A Philosophical Love Story*, *Platonic Excursions*, and *Heidegger und Grund*, but above all: *Erotic Zen*. Herzen also liked *Platonic Excursions*, but said *Goering's Trial* and *Overcoming Hume Through Hume* were his favorites. Neither Jove nor Wallace nor Ellebelle had ever read Calendula. Wallace had tried once, but couldn't complete a single Platonic excursion. Belmonte had read all of Calendula twice, but didn't care for him. (Note: most American critics consider *Heidegger und Grund* to be the richest of Calendula's works, while in Europe, a slim volume called *Emerson: Nietzsche: Power* is thought to be seminal.) Herzen said that Calendula was seven feet tall, had a thick Hungarian accent and the mustache of a circus strongman. M asked Herzen how he had obtained such a specific and certain image of their favorite reclusive philosopher, and Herzen said that it was obvious if you contextualized his writing...and M didn't know whether to congratulate Herzen on this response, or whether to sock him in the mouth.

People came closer, they would speak once or twice, and then they would peel off into the single attribute to remember them by: Wallace and Ellebelle would be the people who he knew by the way they woke up together like people who would always wake up *that way* together—like people who were planning to wake up together, *that way*, forever.

And it wasn't because he thought they were in love—though they might have been—but because he knew that they liked how it felt to let the rest of the world fall to meaningless pieces around them, while they focused on what the other was thinking, or whether they had enjoyed sex that night, or dinner, or that movie Wallace had rented in Williamsburg the day before.

M wondered if in ten years Ellebelle and Wallace would still speak to each other. It would be strange, he thought, if they didn't— because you don't forget all that naked flesh; you don't forget the feeling of a transparent, luminous, fucked-up creature trembling in your arms—the feeling of a pink anus-mouth opening at the presentation of your fingertip, or of lips and teeth fighting back against your mouth, or a barely human voice calling out for mercy and joy...

Only Shakespeare is innocent and wise simultaneously: everyone else has to choose which one they want to be...

(These distinctions and ratios are pointless though, I know, because at the center of a soul flows a river of unmindfulness, and all I have to do is jump in and let the current take me away...)

Lena asks Belmonte for a cigarette.

Belmonte starts to talk about cosmic silence and the eruption of the ordinary in the midst of the extraordinary...

Lena receives a cigarette from Belmonte and dangles it from her lips without lighting it, looking at me, expecting me to answer the question she will never actually ask.

Belmonte says faith, not hope, is all that matters in religious life.

Jove laughs from the futon...

And what would Mallarme's flower be if it were to be inserted into the blankness of our lives at this very moment?—just a sign of the sadness that pervades people and shoots through them like fluorescent light—

"Belmonte, can I ask you a question?"

"As Wittgenstein[24] said..."

"Do you know what M's thinking about when he doesn't have anything to say? During his silences...during his ridiculous pensées—"

"That's easy, Lena: human suffering...the brown moon like a paperbag...your breasts...Lou-Andreas Salomé—"

"And how do you know that Belmonte?—"

"The *Tractatus*[25]—the last line—look it up."

"*Belmonte*—"

"Lena, if you want to know what M is thinking, just ask him."

"So that's the answer then—"

"That's the answer."

Lena went to the bathroom and closed the door, and without lifting the toilet-seat up, she sat down and put her head in her hands.

She was tired of the spring: she wanted to skip right over summer to late autumn, when things were beautifully dying again.

24 One of Calendula's most astute remarks: "Wittgenstein said that consciousness is like the eye that surveys its surroundings, the limit of the world, not a part of it; love is the refutation of Wittgenstein. Love is the eye in the world that looks in on us."

25 Back in his own apartment, Belmonte was reading about the death of Trakl and thinking about the wings of dead dragonflies. At the same time, Jove was thinking about holy men and rosewater and the dreamlike aspect of Art. Wallace was thinking about a blond woman he had spoken to on the train the previous Tuesday who had invited him to get off the train with her at the Lorimer Avenue stop and how only cowardice had stopped him. Belmonte, if he could have received Wallace's thoughts across the hallway would have said, "All the flowers in your garden are dead." Jove would have said that the blond woman was Wallace's Other, and M would have mentioned something about that Stevens poem on the inadequacy of landscapes. M, Jove, and Wallace all considered poetry an act of imaginative renewal. Belmonte considered poetry an essentially philosophical act designed to replace political ideas with sexual anthropology. Belmonte, M, Jove, and Wallace all considered poetry to be preferable to death. None of them considered death to be preferable to even the most inadequate landscapes. On one wall of his bedroom, Belmont had written an equation for deciding whether the soul was awake. At the end of the equation was the conclusion: "star tree no hope anymore Mount Asama!"

She wanted cold winds: piercing, ruinous, deconstructing winds.

"Happiness[26] is not only happiness," she thought, "it's a form of recognition—which is terrifying."

Back in the living room, Belmonte thought of Lena as a faded flower that M had gathered—without understanding the beauty for which he'd picked and ruined it.

26 Still, she loved taking him gently in her mouth while he talked to her, while he told her the most disgusting things that he could imagine. It was reflexive, simple, degrading... unembarrassed: when he came, she would swallow him with such quivering happiness that she would be unable to speak for hours, so that she would just have to lay her head on his stomach, while he continued to talk about things that moved him to cry and thought about women whom she would never know.

27

You look like a rose my little fox and the petals of you grow around me the calyx of your flower and it is so beautiful the way we are born and flower and die my little fox just like the way your lovers grow like slender petals around the memory of me only to shed themselves like shadows splayed across a pool of water and you're sinking away from me into the dark and I can still hear you cry in our little hotel room (you didn't think I noticed?) when I told you I couldn't make love to you and your loneliness bloomed right there like a moon on water and don't you realize how exquisite life is? with its swoons and separations and silences and o' how I want to be smothered and asphyxiated and ruined by life (the tenderness of you clinging to me making me gasp the scent of the rain in that church that we ran into trying to stay dry and the sound of the church organ underneath us and the holiness of you there besides me no longer separate from the rain and the music and everything)

She writes to me: she says that she's waiting for me; that she's been waiting—that we'll never meet. She just wants someone who does not want to go *beyond* writing—thus the chalk moon; the radius of a circle; the spectral evasions of self and soul.

I reread her letters whenever I feel myself closing up or growing cold—her words have an internal kinetic *something* that I need (like water and air and music and sunlight)...

And so she lives in a liminal space within me; the woman I've never met; the woman whose London address was written inside a used copy of *The Recognitions*.

And the idea of making love to Joanna is incomprehensible, for obvious reasons—and she says that it's impossible that we'll ever see each other—that we'll only know each other as erasures on a white page.

And she writes to me and says that she is a "sad, colorless individual."

I write and say that "No Joanna: *you are luminescent.*"

For weeks, we will not write anything—then five letters in a day. Then the letters will stop for awhile. One parallel[27] swerves into the other.

When her letters touch my hands, I must apply cotton to soak up the blood.

We want oblivion like an unlit lake: bodies without consciousness: the human strata turned to ash.

---

27   "German is my mother tongue and as such more natural to me, but I consider Czech much more affectionate, which is why your letter removes several uncertainties; I see you more clearly, the movements of your body, your hands, so quick, so resolute, it's almost like a meeting." – Franz Kafka, *Letters to Milena*

i don't know whether this is wise but i can't sleep and so...it wasn't strictly true what i...i know intimacy not physical intimacy but intimacy i do...although, in my social circle and my parents' social circle you aren't encouraged to speak of yourself in fact it's bad form to...it's all hypotheticals and impersonal queries and it's deeply unsettling but it allows me to get away with all manner of atrocious...it's not important but i do want to tell you that...i know it might seem perverse the way that i...well, my father calls it self-abnegation...what i'm working on it's...emphatically bound to purity the idea of purity the practice of purity and not purity of heart is to will one thing no purity of heart is to will several things and not know which is the truer better thing and to worry about this forever no not...it's...i want to collate what one imagines it to be before one first hears the word but...wyatt and his sapphires... circling a shoreline...and you quoting porete to me not thinking i'd grasp what you...please don't think i'm without courage that i'm comfortable that i'm perfectly safe that i'm not tap-dancing across a courtyard surrounded by snipers it's not...it's laster and his one true piano key the missing note the non-entity orpheus without a myth it's impossible and yet sometimes i believe i'm almost...my solitude remains entirely untouched and i will give it away but i will give it away only once and i won't be afraid when i do

They were listening to *Court and Spark,* but keeping it very low because Wallace was asleep, and because it was very late.

Because she was unable to sleep, Ellebelle had joined them in the living room.

"Joni always makes me want to cry uncontrollably," Ellebelle said.

Herzen came back in from the hallway, where he had been reading.

"This record reminds me of the sword fight in *Savage Detectives,*" Herzen said.

"What the hell are you talking about Herzen?" M asked.

"You'll understand me when you've read the book—"

"I've read it three times you idiot—"

"Well, read it again."

"The only proper literary critic is the critic who is willing to be considered an idiot by his contemporaries," Belmonte said, following Herzen into the living-room from the hallway, yawning, another (presumably Irish) coffee in his hands.

"Every damned day I wake up with the craziest dreams in my head," Jove said. "I hate when it gets late, because then I'm too close to the Dream World for comfort..."

"Dreams are the beginning of the end of the beginning of moral life, at least, that's how I interpret Nietzsche," Belmonte offered for context.

"Belmonte, you read Nietzsche too much like a Nietzschean—" Herzen said, "he should be read like a Heideggerian."

"Herzen—that's the stupidest shit I've ever heard," Belmonte said, waving his cigarette hand in front of Herzen's face in disgust. "I don't even know what that's supposed to mean."

"Sure you do Belmonte—it means that you interpret one writer through the system of another...and not the other way around."

"Yes, but Heidegger has more than one system, and his systems contradict each other—and his systems draw upon Nietzsche's systems in the first place...it's like trying to solve a koan with a jigsaw puzzle."

"Somewhere, Democritus is scuttling along with a crutch and a stick, smoking a cigarette, going—what the hell happened to philosophical honesty..." M said.

There was this fringe of happiness around everything, M thought, a beautiful variableness and uncertainty to conversation (the uncertainty of being alive) that was like a tuba breaking in at a ballet recital.

"I think I have a point—" Belmonte said, annoyed and vaguely determined.

"Can you guys flip the record over?—" Ellebelle asked, a request to which Jove dutifully acceded.

"The dialectical process is kind of Agnes Martinesque...*por entre los barrotes pone el punto fiscal...*" Belmonte said.

"What a lamentable family of exhausted, ridiculous drunks this is—" M sighed.

"See!—" Jove said, interrupting M, "this is the problem with all you damned IN-TELLECT-U-ALS: *the enfeeblement of sensuality...* so let's not pretend this disagreement is anything other than the general problem of American bohemian life—the loss of everything sacred except for the blow-job or the beautiful FUCK with a stranger drunk on white wine, or Papst Blue Ribbon...the damned *shanti, shanti, shanti* of painting the emptiness with clouds..."

"Belmonte's just loaded," Ellebelle said, rolling her eyes.

"He ain't drunk, Elle, he on some Other shit."

"I assure you that I'm only blitzed...and partially more sinned against than sinning, but definitively and logically (according to Aristotle's method) not drunk..."

M stood up and stretched, a cup of chamomile tea still warm at his feet.

"I wish I could be the lies I tell—" M said laconically, "because then I could be myself...or is that just what we're all thinking right now? God it's late—we should really put on some more coffee..."

"Don't be dramatic—" Herzen said to M, frowning. "You get so dramatic whenever we run out of coffee. It's like Ibsen all the time with you buddy when your caffeine runs out—"

"In his sermons the Buddha left the nature of the gods undecided. The ultimate truth, though, *aramartha*, is a state of inner experience by means of noble wisdom, *aryavijna*..." Belmonte trailed off and closed his eyes. "It is beyond the ken of words..."

Wallace, who had woken up due to Belmonte's yawn, entered the living room in his pajamas.

"Hey, dudes—what are you all doing awake?"

"The ambiguity of symbols..." Belmonte mumbled, "comes from their distance from us in space and time...the first utterance of a new idea is always perfectly clear—but after that...who knows?—"

"How can you say that?—about symbols..." Herzen asked Belmonte angrily. "It's like you're just stringing together whatever incoherent ideas pop into that prodigal head of yours..."

"*I just know, ok?*—and it's what my algorithm predicts, anyway—"

"What algorithm?"

"Hey, is someone gonna put on coffee?—" Wallace asked, "there's no way I'm falling asleep now."

"A system for encoding bullshit Herzen, like your poetry—"
Feet shuffling.

"Wanna have some coffee with me Elle?"

"Maybe..." Ellebelle said; sniffly, puffily.

Wallace kissed her on the forehead, leaning down.

"You little monkey."

"Banana fucker," Ellebelle said.

"Shit eater."

"Do you ever hear the depths of multiple silences?" M inquired of no one in particular.

"I have—" Herzen said, "it's the silence of poetry itself."

"Multiple depths means multiple deaths," Belmonte intoned.

M drank the last of his chamomile tea, and immediately wished that he had made more.

"But what gets me really, isn't the idea of nothingness, which is at worse benignly terrifying, but the idea of becoming a corpse. Now that *fucking* scares me, becoming a corpse..."

"M you are way too DAMNED scared of dying for someone who reads so much philosophy."

"I don't read that much Jove..."

"All you do is read that shit—all DAMNED day—if you aren't on your typewriter, talking to your DAMNED self..."

"I guess."

"You know, Heidegger says something about that—" Herzen interrupted helpfully, "about our own sense of decay...being within that decay, living within it, fully aware of our our own spiral decline towards nothingness..."

This made Jove lean back with a reflective sigh.

"Being dust or ashes isn't so bad...but being a pile of decaying bones and guts—now that's some crazy SHIT—"

"Elle where are the coffee grounds?" Wallace asked from the stove.

"Hey M—where is Lena tonight?" Herzen asked.

"I have no idea," M said.[28]

He was lying.[29]

28 Belmonte lit another cigarette to compete with the two he already had going (one in each hand). Wallace walked into the living room reading a copy of *Gödel, Escher, Bach*—an event so funny that Belmonte crumpled to the floor at once with laughter. Later, Herzen found Jove and Belmonte smoking at the windowsill—talking about proofs they'd come up with in favor God's existence. "God's a crazy bitch—" Jove said, "because we all know that GA-HD-DD is a WO-MAN."

29 "And that's it—" M said, "that's the problem—right now, the only faith that anyone has is faith in the emptiness of life.""Faith is wanting to screw somebody until you both can't fucking breathe—" Herzen said.

Jove and M were the only ones still awake.

Jove noticed that every few minutes M would take a piece of paper from his pocket, unfold it three or four times, quickly scan it left to right with his eyes, and put it back in his pocket before continuing to write in his notebook.

"M..."

"Yes Jove—"

"What the HELL are you reading over and over and over and over?"

"Jesus, you're gonna wake everyone up Jove...it's nothing."

"Fine, I'll be quiet—" Jove hissed, "but you have to tell me what's in that crazy-ass cryptogram..."

"It's just something that's made me think a little bit."

"About WHAT?"

M closed his notebook and looked at Jove.

"The person who volunteers to be the safety-net during my existential high-wire act."

"*Shit,* that's a cop-out if I ever heard one..."

"Well, I'm sorry, but it's something private...I mean—it's nothing that anyone could understand—like anything with me— it's internalized..."

"Oh, don't be so mopey—"

"Look Jove—I can't show you the letter."

"I don't need to read your DAMNED letter, I just wanted to know what was keeping you awake."

"Well, what's keeping *you* awake Jove?"

"M—what's keeping me awake is how much I don't want to die."

"Well, that's what's keeping me awake too."

"Well *hell*—" Jove said, slapping M on the back, "why didn't you tell me?"

"Because you knew it already, because that's the whole

reason we're friends in the first place. And I'll tell you something, Jove—this particular letter isn't what matters—it's what it sparks in me; it's what it opens up in me, that matters—at least to me. It's just one of many weapons that I've hurled against the frozen sea inside of me to try to break it open—"

"*DAMN*—"

"But Jove—*Jove*—you knew that already."

"I know, I'm just testing you M…*shit*—"

"Because if a person can't do that, can't break open that…"

"Then what—?"

"Well then…" M lowered his voice to a whisper and pointed to Wallace and Ellebelle's room, "then you end up in some endless Nietzschean reoccurrence—you end up living a life without any hopeful intentions—you end up falling to the bottom of the void you've been dropped into at birth, instead of climbing back out…"

"You really think that's where you're heading?—do you really think that's where *they are*?"

"Who knows Jove?—I'm just saying…"

"Because that's why they don't like you—because they think you judge them…"

"Well doesn't everyone judge everyone? Isn't that what life is about—making judgements—I mean…"

"No, you're right M—we all do it."

"Then what's your point Jove?"

"I'm just explaining your reality back to you so that you don't have any *ill*-usions—"

"You would have to do more than *that* to divest me of my illusions, Jove…believe me—I cling to them like life-rafts—I float back and forth across a sublime ocean on them, Jove—it's really fantastic—*io promesso*—"

"And what does this letter have to do with your illusions?"

"Oh, that's easy—it makes me think that my illusions might not be illusions, but that they're actually improbable truths…that the soul exists, that moral life is real and complex, that aesthetic life is as real and complex as moral life...and that people can go beyond basic communication and really feel some kind of empathy, Jove—my God—"

"M it's four in the morning—dammit—you'll wake everyone up with that kinda talk."

M smiled.

"Oh come on Jove—you were waiting for a speech from me."

Jove laughed loudly enough that they both heard Ellebelle (it had to be Ellebelle) bang a fist against the dividing wall in an attempt to hush them.

"M I'm always waiting for speeches from you. You're nothing but fuck-*ing* speeches, like a prince in goddamn Shakespeare, his pockets stuffed full of Rhetorick."

"I'm out of good speeches tonight Jove."

"*Hell*—I've noticed."

Lena walking around Williamsburg with her hands on her head, humming Berlioz crazily...white flowers opening in the postrain predawn...M closed his eyes, suddenly feeling exhausted:

"What I'm trying to do Jove, is square a few genuine experiences against the experience of wanting genuine experiences—trying to parse for myself what has been real and what are the things that I've really just been hoping are real; I'm trying to squeeze the fantastical nonsense out of my mind like dirty water from a wet rag—I'm just trying to let the light of life shine through me like it'll shine through the living room window in about two fucking hours—because *Jove, Jove, Jove*—everything is poison in this city, and I'm just beginning to realize it... everything and everyone...and the worst part is that I'm chronically inclined to like people, to like almost everyone I meet—in one way or another—even the people who obviously don't like me—and they are legion—I mean, Jesus Jove—think about those two..." M gestured again at Wallace and Ellebelle's door. "But it lacks meaning—at least—life lacks meaning if you don't let it cause you a little pain...and I'm talking about the spaces that open up between people—I'm saying that we need to accept humane longing, a humane kind of suffering in order to close those gaps...to have togetherness...to have love. We all want to be born out of ourselves—to have the parts of ourselves that we don't want to die—and that's why I'm up late, reading a letter, waiting for the moon's astonished eyes to close—because I can't let myself go to sleep until I really understand what exactly is so dissatisfying about my life on one hand, and what's so ecstatic about it on the other...because I know that there's this place beyond love[30] where nothing wants to be born—where everyone has recovered the meaning they lost as children...and literally—*sure*—this is silly... it sounds crazy, but—"

Jove shook his head.

"I GET IT—"

"Siehe, wir lieben nicht, wie die Blumen, aus einem einzigen Jahr," M recited. "You'll give in to it too Jove: the ecstatic mode of nostalgia."

"Hell M—nostalgia is the name I paint on the pedestal of beauty—*shit*," Jove[31] said.

30 "Love is severe, mocking, exacting. It will not let us exist as we are. Love demands a revolution in consciousness."

31 As M once explained to Jove: a person only knows they're a writer once they begin to continue the chapters of their favorite novels after those novels end (changing all the names, places, events, times, characters, timbres, tones, colors, textures, styles, and techniques, but only very slightly). M also said that being an artist meant trying to sculpt water into something lovely before it reached the drain. Jove said that this was bullshit because art was just electrons meeting and exploding indeterminately, so that waves of energy could spread through the universe at the velocity of light, and that the purpose of the artist was to convert matter into energy like a worm converting food scraps into soil; that beauty was drained of its force completely if beauty got tangled up with material; with physical stuff...in the end, they agreed that the artist should be like Satie sitting at the piano, dabbing at drops of rain, but neither M nor Jove knew how they had arrived at that conclusion.

...here[32] we are and I'm underdressed and feel as though I've run up fifty flights and I don't know; I've just woken up, it's eight a.m. and I'm writing this before I've had much of a chance to think about it or you or the train I have to catch. I wanted to write to you (for some time) because it was like you knew somebody I knew a poem but a poem can be a person and it wasn't a poem was it? It was a moment...I wanted to write to you because I couldn't do what I truly wanted to do (share a glance across a room, pass by you in a corridor, &c.) and...how does one do that with words? I don't know. I'm trying. I'm trying...I thought of you last night because I had a passionate disagreement with someone and I cannot partake in a passionate disagreement without wanting to scream HOW LONG IS IT SINCE YOU'VE SEEN THE SUN RISE and I love I love the way you withhold periods at the end of your sentences like you're afraid to close the gate or you just don't want to and I think if I knew you better I would be able to squint at the white space and I'd see that the sentence runs on and on and on until it folds back on itself like a möbius strip...and let's write but let's not write about love because I...it's my life's ambition to become shklovsky truth be told "moving diagonally like a knight, I have intersected your life" and "take your heart in your teeth, write a book" yes, a prohibition against writing about love, you'll forgive me...I read to construct monuments of myself, you know, me17thdec04 me21stfeb11 &c. points in my past I distributed myself at... drop-offs, you understand I know you do...I can go back to collect myself should I need to it's the only life insurance there is...you cannot attach safety lines to those you love it's...you wouldn't tether your father to yourself then scale the side of a mountain without some sort of harness it isn't advisable it's basic mountaineering 101 but people do they do M I've seen them it's 1:27a.m. I thought I was fearful or weak-hearted or that "passion's a precipice so won't you please move away move away please" was the epigraph to my existence but I was mistaken it takes years years

---

32 My response: "Written kisses don't reach their destination, rather they are drunk on the way by the ghosts."

years for eyes to adjust it's 1:29a.m. I'm writing from the outskirts of sleep
I'm writing to you as I would write to myself and nothing is mortifying
nothing is contemptible because I've written all this before and as walser's
fräulein says to jakob I am dying of the incomprehension of those who
could have seen and held me I am dying of the emptiness of cautious and
clever people and it's beautiful isn't it not to want anything anymore yes
it is beautiful and when I thought of you I don't know what I thought
just there you were flashing up into my field of vision like one of those
amber collision warnings on the motorway or freeway...it's snowing in
london I read your last bottle rocket four times in a row (me19thjan13)...

Whenever he woke up, Jove would write down his dreams in a ridiculous, oversized notebook that he had made for himself out of construction paper and tape and glue.

Jove had dreams about almost everything: willow leaves, Africa (and its imaginary landscapes), killer robots, saints, witch-doctors, childhood, dying (physical, sexual, aesthetic, mystical), limbo, the riddles of Averroës...thunderstorms (which he was afraid of), music (songs he had yet to write or had already written), Nature, the end of the world, sex (anal/homosexual), transformations (between human and divine)...

Jove thought that the spirit was like water, jostling to make its own movements sing.

Water leveled everything: it flowed through his whole body. One had to break through the enclosure of the other—one had to realize that the terrible Satori of the bohemian life was just another false sense of enlightenment—or reality.

Jove was born with a sadness that he couldn't quite root out of himself, a sadness that would simply transcend itself in him every once in awhile: granting him an almost paralyzing clarity of other people—a clarity that he knew the people around him couldn't appreciate.

Waking up was always marked by joy and longing: it made him feel like he was swimming through liquified darkness, or breaking down the geometry of longing. (Vision clouded over by vijana—some shit like that.)

The gross weight of defiance; asking for an absolute encounter—an eternal love...

Of all the people who lived in the apartment—Jove was the most Alone.

O

"...I took a long ride on an omnibus out into the Bronx and back, and saw all the fashion on Fifth Ave. When you see the display of wealth and beauty here, it will make you crawl. It is the most gorgeous city imaginable, beside being at present the richest and most active place in the world. The swarms of humanity of all classes inspire the most diverse of feelings: envy, hate, admiration and repulsion. But truly it is the place to live."

-Hart Crane to his mother, February 19th, 1917.

nto his ninth cup of chamomile tea, watching the stars drain away into the sky's dark infinitive...

And the sky was beginning to look hysterically beautiful, he thought: like skin swelling under the pressure of a fingertip.

Lena was probably painting the same sky from a different angle and singing in French or Spanish or, if she was especially sad, Portuguese.

It was an El Greco morning alright: an El Greco morning of all-too human divinities and symbols—fragile and lachrymose and ecstatic.

Without love, human beings couldn't survive for a single day, and the sun was not disappointing, M noticed—coming up to meet the condition of terrible fluidity imposed on it by the sky.

(And because of the way his voice erased itself with sorrow when he spoke—M appeared to be remembering someone else in a blue scene washed by white rain.)[35]

Three floors down, he could hear Jove singing:

Where have all the graveyards gone? Long time passing
Where have all the graveyards gone? Long time ago
Where have all the graveyards gone? Gone to flower everyone
When will they ever learn? When will they ever learn?

---

35 It doesn't take any courage to stay in bed, but there's a kind of precise art that it takes to do it right: it's very easy to be so heavy with longing that you forget about anything else, so that kitchen or hallway (let alone the city at large) seems infinitely far away, as if you're actively engaged in Zeno's paradox, never getting closer, never getting further away. Love is only embarrassing to people who cannot love: I'll say that. But this is the justification for my own life: finite human truth blooming early in the May morning. New York displays its false disarray as proof of authenticity. I'm searching, searching, searching:

He wanted to hold her hand, and she wouldn't let him because she was afraid to ruin the elegance of late spring with emotion, and because she couldn't bear to feel weak around him—above all.[36]

Every time he would see her, he would ask, can't things be simple? or why can't they be? And she would just tell him (as she always did) that they couldn't be because they were born in the wrong alignment, and that he had to hop over Hadrian's wall seventeen times before they could fall in love, and that she had forgotten to bathe in beeswax—and that was why she couldn't kiss him, anyway.

M knew that Lena had to love him in her own magical/unmagical way—that she would never let him see the paintings she never showed anyone, and that it would never really matter, anyway, how unfortunate things were between them—because she drew their love like Escher, and painted it like Klee.

And it was awful the way they messed up this love of theirs: the unfinished sentences, the understanding despite everything—[37]

36 On the rare days Lena would allow him to see her, they would fall right away into their strange way of talking to one another, sentences that stopped midway, or sometimes after just a word because the other could always anticipate what was going to be said. It was as if the time they spent together was happening in some parallel world where everything outside of them was separate and unimportant compared to the esoteric dialogue that flowed back and forth between them, like a wave of light.

37 Why do you provide for me nothing when I ask you for substance? A few remarks on silence. How love reveals ethics. How love denies ethics. How love is a vacuum for ethics. How hope is the syllogism of a liar. How all Cretans are liars. How every surface is invisible to the hand travelling over it (which can never reveal the wave-like ripple that is the first circle of the outer circle of which the surface is a part).

He grows up in an old house; the upstairs bathroom has yellow tiles; it overlooks a garden; in the summer he likes to sit in the bathtub and listen to the rain and watch the peculiar light that skates across the yellow bath tile.

He can spend entire summer afternoons reading in the bathtub; autumn afternoons are even better, and his life has no irreversible tragedies: no one he knows has ever died, and he is sure, as a matter of fact, that he will never die himself.

To adults, he has a lackluster, disorganized personality—he is precocious but distant: floating down an interior river, waving to the people standing on the banks.

He begins to write poems that resemble the infinite chain of days—he peoples his imagination with dead princes from Greek tragedy; fragments of glass flowers; with pathos and shadows like in the Rembrandts he will later see in Paris.

He wants to live inside an impressionist painting or old Vienna; his poems become colder—like a white dress in moonlight—but he is no longer sure of himself by this point...

Swallows dart through the spaces between trees and stars, he moves to Brooklyn, hangs out with Jove, meets Belmonte, starts a novel, throws it away, starts it again; throws it away again.

He finds an address inside a novel and begins a correspondence with a woman he will never meet...

Further back in time, he is still imagining his future self more romantically than it will turn out—he has yet to meet La Rondine; he has yet to feel the ecstasy of falling through an invisible trapdoor into Nowhere.

The great chains of myth fascinate him—but he's not sure whether they have any place in the life around him—i.e.—a season's dying is no longer associated with anything other than his own, internal consciousness of the divine...

Nondescript trees, houses falling apart, children playing

on swing sets—the noise of the ice cream truck—and later Jove's prayer circles, Wallace's band practices, Ellebelle's handknit sweaters, the inconsistency of the L train, talking about Calendula's books with Herzen at late-night diners...copying the aphorisms of Wittgenstein and Lichtenberg into the margins of his notebook; creating an asystematic system of being by which to live—by which to cope with living...creating a loneliness out of the divisions apparent in the self, revising those divisions like he is rewriting a long, silent sentence...[38]

38 He comes home and showers—hoping to get out of the apartment before anyone else is awake. He tapes an envelope to his bedroom door in case Lena comes by looking for him; he hopes that Belmonte won't read it and change the text, like he sometimes does...*I got your missive last night: water sprung from an ark. A whitewash of shadow and lye. Can you get your body back to obeying pain? can you tack the nerve to the inside of its sheath? apply pressure to the wound at the center of your indifference? Your consonants are always summer and night. Agape is a motion through freefall. Now it is possible that the structure of a dancing body is prophetic; that receptivity is a semantic aim, and Lena, you know that already... 'Kiss me, wrap me around your bones...'—this is what you'll say. And I won't be back today, or maybe I will; I don't know; but don't be upset (because I know how upset you get)—*

I only visit you when it rains, though it has rained often lately, so that I am drawn to you again and again, like a ruined moth fluttering about some distant light, drawn to the way you smoke those hand-rolled cigarettes and lounge about the bed like some Egyptian goddess, and demand that I leave, that I must, that you're in no mood today, and of course I nod my head and leave without a word, and the rain goes on for hours while I think of you, and the way that you smell, and the dampness of the room, and the pink peeling wallpaper, and the taste of ash and mint in your mouth.[39]

39 And when you come back in the evening, M, like a pathetic wilted flower, I laugh and tell you that I had never meant for you to leave, that you don't know anything about women, and I smoke, I saunter up to you and kiss you on the neck, standing on tiptoes, and I breathe deeply so that my chest expands and presses against you, and I run my hand along your side, and you are so prim and polite that you do not move, no you do not smile or say a thing, and slowly, as if I were not there, you remove your hat and raincoat, and your wet shoes and socks, almost amused at your own stoicism, like a wolf at the door.

I've tried to write Lena down for years, but she is still not real to me, with her red lipstick, and African dresses, and the occasional female lover who I find tracing a finger down across her navel and through her pubic hair; kissing her softly on the mouth—

I can't get past this first scene: colorful paintings hanging in the sun, Lena making coffee on the stove, mixing the grounds, humming love songs to herself—so completely aware/unaware of her charm—and me: still laying on the bed, half-asleep, aching with tenderness and joy and stupid, stupid sentimentality...

But I can't describe the smell of the coffee, the texture of the sunlight in spring (it has to be spring)—or the trace of her hips swaying through a whiteish slip.

I can't even quite describe how her dark fleshy lips taste, or how her skin feels like mud spread thinly across a smooth stone, or how we used to lay naked side by side without touching[40] for hours, just to see if we could make each other cum by reading each other's thoughts (which was impossible but which we both swore happened once).

Lena is the dream of my art: everything that is impossible in words; flesh and sweat and the stench of a big, beautiful body. She will never be real, I know that now. But I am still in love with her grace—

40 She likes the sensation of my tongue slipping inside of her, my fingers dimpling the muscles on her back, spreading her legs apart. She likes how we make art together. How we gorge on roses and morning coffee too weak to wake us up, but strong enough to purify us. We pull each other apart like dandelions; we work ourselves down to the flowerless stem where all we can do is laugh and imagine that we are asleep.

And I know that I'll go, as the scene continues, and that the coffee will be drunk black, and that she will not let it cool, and that in the afternoon it will rain and I will knock on her door and she will reject me.

I am not real enough for her either...I want to open the world of her at the core...

I want plain myrtle for the crown of her sex: for the unraveling of her body from the erotic spool.

Like most mornings, they were sitting around, waiting for someone to fry up some eggs, comparing Pynchon to Gaddis, and wondering whether real comprehension would simply appear above them like Plato's third man, or whether they would really have to earn it.

"I dreamt that I lived inside a tree in Prospect Park," Jove said.

"I don't believe in the efficacy of metaphors," Belmonte explained, "which are all dreams really are."

"Literature is nothing but horrors," Jove cried. "Tragedy and motherfuckin' lamentations. Odysseus killing a hundred suitors. Hamlet throwing the whole damned court of Elsinore to the damned dogs."

"Y me retiró hasta azular, y retrayéndome endurezco, hasta apretarme el alma," Belmonte sighed.

"Wisdom is the opium of the flaccid," M, who had just gotten out of the shower and was still in a towel, said.

M, seeing that everyone was hoping for fried eggs, went straight to the stove.

Ellebelle was already there, working on a coffee carafe.

Herzen burst in, wearing the same clothes he had been wearing the night before. M wondered where Herzen had slept, if he had slept at all.

"I've decided I'm going to go to law school...fuck literature," Herzen announced dramatically.

"That's a good attitude. Very practical," M said lazily.

Belmonte smiled approvingly.

"That's where entropy leads: you create a system and it breaks down into something less dignified...so bravo Herzen."

Ellebelle came over and put the coffee carafe on the coffee table and sat down next to Herzen on the futon.

Wallace came in, apparently awake, and told everyone that they should order Chinese food for breakfast—a proposal which was seconded by none.

Wallace saw Herzen had put his hand on Ellebelle's thigh.

"You know, if you think about it," M said from the stove, "the last system to resist entropy successfully was Dante's...Dante was the last person who knew how to ascend from hell to heaven in order—the last person who knew what his priorities were... now the pilgrim's journey is all mixed up...fragments of heaven and hell and purgatory lying around like bits of broken glass."

"Scattered clouds, an unfinished novel, a city in rebellion..."

"Belmonte, do you ever listen to what other people say, or do you just *TALK*?—" Jove asked.

"Do you know what it is to have a soul?—Jove?—it is only to know that we die and go away forever...once you remember that, then you've earned your soul. And a soul, therefore, can be won or lost at anytime...*Engel!: es wäre ein Platz, den wir nicht wissen, und dorten, auf unsäglichem Teppich, zeigten die Liebenden...*"

"*But the soul, the soul,*" M thought while flipping over a pathetic looking egg.

"We only love what of ourselves we see in other people," Jove said quietly.

"Today I was thinking about how being in love is like tying your own hands together so tightly that they're drained of blood...so that you can't feel them anymore...so you can see them turning blue," Herzen said, looking only at Ellebelle.

"The dust on the futon right now is starting to make me cough," Ellebelle complained. "This place is filthy and the typewriter sounds like a hundred apples being bitten into at once."

M rolled his eyes.

"What more is needed from a writing device?—the sorrow of angels?—I mean this is the sound of art being made—right Herzen?—"

(No one knew if M was being sarcastic.)

Jove stood up suddenly, struck by a new idea.

"To love in the way we are accustomed to now, is to take our emptiness and fill it up with another kind of damned EMPTY-NESS...love must be stupid, animal, crude, violent, tender, funny—it must be the intensification of every damned thing we feel—*all at once.*"

Everyone looked at Belmonte, expecting a response, only to realize that Belmonte had fallen asleep in place, Indian style, on the floor.

M, aware that it was now up to him to say something, put down his spatula and turned off the stove.

"I always thought that all our sins came from love and that's what made them forgivable; that the forgiveness in the best literature is always an admission that we fell only because we tried to leap, like Quixote, or Hamlet, or Lear...and that's what tragedy is, I think...a mad leap on the wings of language. Seeking love and finding hatred or death or absurdity instead, or all of those things at once...or maybe tragedy is just the expression of human laziness and inertia—I think about that too sometimes—"

"M, are the eggs done yet?—" Herzen asked. "I've been hungry since I woke up."

"To be contemporary is to have given up completely on love—" Jove said.

"Rubens, who loved fat girls, as I'm sure you know..." Belmonte, suddenly awake, said, pointing to an invisible spot between Jove's eyes with his cigarette. "This strange creature, if you will—which is the brothel-museum-dream—is where one finds all the strands of Baudelaire. But here's an important point—" Belmonte continued, pointing to his own forehead, "that dream corresponds to a real and rather magical place in Paris: the Palais-Royal eighteenth-century garden and colonnade...but look: all of you are too worried about M's almost certainly terrible fried eggs to pay attention to me, so I'll shut up—"

Jove closed his eyes.[41]
M served the eggs in a pizza box.

41 Jove had wanted to spend the early part of the morning (the only good part) writing down his dreams—which were more plural and various than he ever told anyone, including M. Jove had a recurring dream where he was lost in a desert of broken glass. The thing about the glass was that when it cut you, it drew no blood, so that the further Jove walked, and the more he slipped and fell, the more he appeared like a ragged linen cloth. Jove always woke up just when the white of bone was beginning to show. What Jove feared most was never waking up from this dream. (Belmonte's eyes, Jove thought, were like those dreams. You wanted to wake up from them as soon as you fell into them.) Jove wished Belmonte hadn't joined them.

She jumps off the Brooklyn Bridge, he hauls her back in. She moves to Japan, lives in a Buddhist temple all summer, collects butterflies. He says "you give me courage" and she says "New York makes me unhappy" and he says "you might be a sunflower or a moonrock or the face of Brutalist concrete, but I'll still love you"—and she doesn't care.

She takes his manuscript from the garbage and publishes it with a small press where it wins an award.

They break open vessels of kindness, belief, longing; dust, noise, silence.

They pass notes back and forth like clouds.

He writes a new sequence of poems. She burns them. He says they were better than the poems he published, but she doesn't care—the Brooklyn Bridge—a leap; poetry on fire; a Japanese garden.

(She tells him that she wants him to plunge her into the void.)

41

You are like the tree, sheltering my brutalized
Form. You are given to a kind of secret,
To metaphors of silence and gloaming.

The tree grows in the innerness. The tree
Grows along the flood-water at the point of Its receding.
The memory of pain is stronger in the heart

Than anywhere. Because I have suffered for
You, I am like a lotus, rippling in the light.
Pluck me again with your breath.[42]

---

42 When Lena stole my poems she said it was like stealing scraps of the sea. In the winter, she would come over and yell at me for no good reason, and threaten to leave me, standing in the doorway, smoking cigarette after cigarette in her wool coat, until I broke down and said I was sorry. (And the last black currants were gone from the bowl—with cream they were rather good—I remember that too: Lena eating currants after we fought. And these things just have a way of happening—of course they do: consciousness is like a deck of cards—one just needs the right suit, the right shuffle, and everything is perfect, even if in the next hand it all goes to shit...)

Sometimes I can find interesting people reading Auden while it rains who tell me what I am thinking: that with history piling up so fast, almost every day is the anniversary of something awful, or that being a writer means arranging my life into an unbreakable vase that can be thrown against a wall over and over and over and never break, or that somehow, the dreariness of being alone can be reduced to a severe lack of imagination rather than lack of libido.

And maybe (not knowing any better) I moved to New York to guarantee myself the happiness of never feeling at home, and of always needing to reach for something transformative and beautiful, and because of certain poems and books and films (self-explanatory), and because New York was still a good place to extract the joy from people and put it into poetry instead of *ennui* or restless dissatisfaction...

The meaning is *the search for meaning*.

La Rondine unraveled the knot of my life. Laid bare the braid of memory in front of me—having undone it. (Now where was she?)

Floating underneath the afternoon sunlight like a raincloud.

You can't understand what joy you give me when you tell me about your love for beauty, she wrote to me once, *too often I can feel my life slipping back without myself.*

Walking along the Highline with other melancholy people, I play a marvelous game[43] with the memories that are always moving through me like air through the trees; blissfully—bright blue—pushing into the purer and purer sky of absolution.

And a rain of fire looks like a bowl of roses tilted upside down, and already I've had my coffee, showered,[44] eaten, shit, eaten again, made eyes with a stranger on the subway—already several poems and novel fragments have been added to my novel of home-rigged myths and Platonic ideas.

And then there's Jove[45] and all the other roughs who still hop on trains and drive through Mexico without passports, with their in-built mythologies of meaning and adventure—people who have *that* presence—*that* Otherness—which sneaks into their letters and poems and songs and conversations.

And an Arabic singer, as Belmonte explains it, might begin with a single melody and end up somewhere completely different two hours later—a place as mesmerizing (or more so) than where she began.

An artist is just trying to get somewhere they aren't already; they're trying to use any tool they have to build a soul stronger than a straw or paper house—because otherwise the soul will throw its best tendencies away for a good fuck or an expensive cigarette.

43 So Ophelia sits around and cries about her father; so the trains carrying vials of our blood crashed into a mountain—people are always coming back to themselves out of the everyday mélange. I wanted to hide my soul under a few layers of secret worlds—I wanted to call love something that compelled life to continue rather than stop dead in its tracks.

44 Anyway, his days in New York were inevitably the same: wake, eat, run, shower. Write, walk, seduce, abandon. Or: wake, abandon, seduce, eat. Or: Abandon, shower, run, seduce. And so on…M thought it was all like an impressionist painting: delicate, glassy, but not so distinct: eat, shower, walk. Sleep, shower, decompose.

45 It was so easy for Jove to think away all the beautiful, isolated intuitions that formed a pattern inside him. Everything used to be significant. Everything used to be infused with God: The Tree of Life, The Bodhi Tree, Yggdrasil, The Burning Bush (intrinsically numinous objects).

A person should feel the tension of a play about to be staged, Jove says, which is exactly how I feel about life in general: one should always be waiting in the wings in the theater, with the audience already in its seats, and the lights about to go up.

The way I see it, the play is what the stage becomes when it becomes aware of its own theatricality—and consciousness is what happens in the brain when it realizes that it's finally onstage, and the performance is about to begin.

Jove says you have a purple aura love, because you are so quiet; but it shines through you anyway, like the light that pours through the trees. And I want to be a part of you, and for this touch to be deep (deep to the very throat of being). And this is the stuff we're made of: tears and green tea leaves (the layer of sweat that covers us after making love). And when we eat watermelon to keep the heat off, it reminds me of that Chekhov story which is so perfect and so sad, because Chekhov understood how terrible beauty is: like metaphysics and Sinatra records and lips like hands; toes which uncurl at the right moment; the dreams that I have while you can't sleep next to me (because you can never sleep while I sleep). And it's so exquisite the way you've opened in me, now that I've left New York for good; now that I have to remember you, just as you were. And I'd like to bite into you again, Lena, like the watermelon, and spit your seeds back onto the ground and let the earth taste our wonderful sorrow. And it wouldn't be like anything, or it would be like all of our metaphors (or like all of our deceptions): tasting you, spitting you back out for good. So come on Lena, remain where you are; let me sketch you in place; draw you like an epigram. And because, after all Lena, you told me once that you could see an island on the moon whenever it was clear in the sky; because you said that there were extraordinary people there, people who spoke the same language as you, and who were your friends: people you could really talk to and enjoy. (And I still think of you like this, like a butterfly collector in a heaven of butterflies: trying to catch and categorize every single one of them (the butterflies) all at once, when there are really an infinity of butterflies, fluttering through an infinity of time, beyond your comprehension.)

There's a crisis: the crisis of being a complex human being in an uncomplex, homogenous world. (Think of Kafka working at an insurance agency. The frozen sea. The frozen ax.) So we adopt antic dispositions. Maybe.

We find ways of plucking a featherless zen chicken with our minds.

But the language stays the same Horatio, no matter who we're talking to. A river flows by, a fisherman falls into Hericlitus' stream trying to haul in his catch. The core of tragic action, the source of tragic authenticity, is something so irrevocable that no mortal can invent it and no genius can produce it out of thin air. And to love means forfeiting our narcissism—and good riddance!—but the real problem is learning how to love in the first place, of course.

One side of us plunges into self-esteem, the other collapses and reforms as ego—if only to avoid becoming bored or worn-out.

The noise of a sundress sweeps across the floor. Mourning is the one time in our lives when we can avoid being busy little Austrian bureaucrats—and so we have to mourn all the time, *and what we have to mourn is love.*

And more than anything—we overhear ourselves and "just can't believe our ears." It has to do with this hall-of-mirrors sense that there really is no beginning and no end to a book; that it is, like us, as it were—limitless. That's what poems are for, anyway— they become ways of reconciling the ghostly half-present with limitless finitude, or whatever it is that people are always finding just over the horizon of doubt.

And in the fifth act things are different—but how different?—nobody knows.

And dear old Mallarmé: Hamlet of clouds and whispering, Paterian seashells. And Ophelia could be the moon on water, Horatio—just like she is another Antigone at Elsinore.

(A place of radical loss: the abyss of desire: Gauguin's Tahitian girls.)

Knotted up with flowers; the voices of wild ducks at twilight; the sky turning white as a ghost—La Rondine, you were more than a few random, but gorgeous symbols: you were a wonderful gesture in the direction of hope.

Alice was very tall and talked in an almost childish, sing-songy kind of way. They fucked mainly because they were trying to fuse themselves with the feeling of the spring (which was overwhelming that year and caused all sorts of accidents around the city) and because they both believed that desire unfolded backwards in time to include aesthetic infidelity to the lovers that they had loved and lost (or forgotten or simply given up on). M liked Alice's long hair and her large, almost prenaturally moist breasts which he like to play with for hours (seemingly) with his tongue. She was a singer in a jazz band and sometimes he'd go to her gigs and read while she sang (usually a little off-key) always with wonderful, melancholy gusto. What he liked most about Alice, related to, but not reducible to her large, wettish breasts, was the childish joie de vivre she took in lovemaking, and her preference for nudity and dirty words.

*

"Then it occurred to me that Duke Mu's song would have had music and a dance that went with it, too. We don't have the dance, of course. Nor do we have the music, and Chinese musical notation doesn't go back that far. These are the earliest forms of literature, probably, in the world," M explained.

"M, why were you pretending like you didn't see me just now?—while you were crossing the street?—" Alice asked.

"I think I resemble a person holding a flying balloon in his hand with a lead weight chained to his ankle, on the verge of being torn apart by the two contrasting forces," M said sadly, not making eye-contact.

"M, what is that piece of paper in your hands?" Alice asked.

"What is that piece of paper in your hands?" she asked again.[46]

Inwardness was a wound, Alice thought suddenly, looking at M not looking at her. Love was a wound: love was a wound inside the first wound (the wound that opened the first wound wider). M's waywardness was out of her control, and the best thing to do (Alice decided right there on the sidewalk) was to live with a kind of innocent levity that could co-exist with sorrow. There was no point anymore with anything serious: any serious hopes or ideas about the future. A pure thought would always abrogate a motion: a pure thought could stop her cold. Here was birth, here was annihilation: both bound her to Eros like an angel tied to a stone.

She snatched the paper from him.

46 *and you see last night it occurred to me that nabokov mapped one of my most loved novels on a butterfly wing—a pseudophilote i think because white is mentioned sixty eight times and black ninety one times and yellow twenty nine times and blue fifty one times i counted i counted them all and it turns out pseudophilotes are native to switzerland and russia and germany and france and england and every country martin edelweiss touches and i felt sick because of that realisation because i've no right to it i've no right to any realisations i've had in my life i am so so small-souled you wouldn't believe me M nothing has happened to me*

Ellebelle[47] and Wallace were neither meticulous nor crazy in the way that they did or didn't love each other, or the way that they did or didn't make love, which was frequently, but predictably.

They lived with M first for fun,[48] then out of obligation, and then out of inertia (purely), and because otherwise they couldn't have afforded cigarettes and beer and Sunday movies in Manhattan, or paying the cover to see a Canadian noise-rock band, or wasting their time in some loft on Myrtle Avenue, while two graduate students talked about media studies or made out next to them, and things like that.

You had to sacrifice something, they both believed, to be with someone, to stick with them for real, and they both knew that they were still actively trying to figure out what it was exactly that they were going to sacrifice.

Yet, somehow, despite their attempts at sacrifice, or discipline, or whatever it was they were aiming at, they always ended up in someone's loft talking about art until four in the morning and drinking beer they didn't buy themselves and wondering how they were going to get home.

So for obvious reasons, they had begun to think that they should just complete the diagram and move to Berlin for good, if they were gonna keep acting this way: and truth was, *they probably would.*

47 In film school she had lived on $250 a month in an old house with six friends and seven cats, and you could drink beer and coffee and not sleep for days watching Jarmusch films and writing love songs on guitar, and she missed that now: in the city, in a relationship, needing more money than she used to need, and not being free at all to do what she wanted. But the best a person can do, anyway, is insert themselves into details of their life, not the other way around.

48 "Simone Weil is a poet," Herzen says. "Wittgenstein is a poet," Belmonte says. "Jove is a poet," Jove says. "An orchid is a poem," Lena says. Joanna is an orchid, M thinks.

Lena says that her mother is sick—she says that she has to send money home, even though she doesn't have enough for herself. Lena doesn't try to sell her paintings though; it's almost like she doesn't care. Lena is a genius—Lena paints with innocence and grace—Lena will not have any success.

Writing poems or painting[49] is worthless nowadays, to most people—so we sell old books, old records, old clothes; so we make love in the middle of the afternoon when we should be working.

Lena sings at bars, but she's no good. She has a beautiful face though, so she still makes decent tips. Poor Lena, with her harrowing, lonely life. Lena with her beautiful face and paintings that pile up for nothing and no one.

But this is ok, she explains, all this—having a beautiful face, not having any money.

She goes swimming at the YCMA almost every night. She speaks French with tourists and gives Spanish lessons to business women three days a week.

Recently, almost all of her paintings have exclusively employed shades of blue; we carve names on raindrops; we stop taking cabs we can't afford—but we can't stop—but we do; but we can't.

49 The perfection of certain pictures overwhelmed him: Van Gogh's almond blossoms or Kandinsky's seventh composition, or almost anything from Picasso's blue period or one of his clowns or whores. And Lena herself was like a painting, he thought, the waters of her soul flowing over his apartment, her studio; over Brooklyn, and across the water to Manhattan...anyway, it was all just from a novel he was beginning to write...kissing in the grass; letting the afternoons turn to smoke.

I'm the only one who sees through M, or maybe I'm not, it's impossible for me to know anymore, what I feel, or what M feels, or who I am, or who M is; whether I want to paint with colors or shadows or if I just want to draw fanciful old men on the backs of napkins, and drink coffee in the afternoon heat rising off Irving Avenue, where M and I go to get cheap coffee and sandwiches at Cafe Verde.

I keep begging M to rent us a cheap hotel room so that we don't have to hear his roommates talk or worry about getting walked in on, but whatever money he makes he keeps for himself, or for rent, or whatever it is he spends his money on; doing philosophical housework like reading Derrida or conducting dialectics with Belmonte or getting drunk with Herzen and singing Russian folk songs...

And that's M's problem—that he can't commit himself to anything except fragments, and that the more he tries to love me, the more he forces me into a non-Euclidean room full of emotional moonlight.

And M is always going on and on, talking about nights in the country as a child; skies full of stars; Emerson and baseball and a hundred other bits of Americanized romanticism[50] that makes me wanna throw up—but it is romantic too: orange sherbet and radio oldies and milkshakes and bicycle rides—that sorta thing.

When he met me, I was living in Williamsburg and making paintings I never sold, and paying more money than I

50 I slept with M the first night we met. I remember waking up with him after his roommates had gone to work and watching him make coffee on the stove and how intently he listened to the record he put on, something by Bach I think, or maybe it was Beethoven, I forget. He was very lovely I thought, so quiet and obscure, stirring the dingy pot by himself while I took a shower and got dressed and ate the oatmeal he had also made for me...the coffee was very strong, I guess he didn't filter the grounds, just made it cowboy style, and I remember sitting on the floor (they didn't have a kitchen table) drinking the coffee with him, looking into his eyes, thinking how intimate this all was, and how perfect.

could afford for rent, and thinking that *polemos* and *logos* were the same, binding everything together, creating a unity where there was only ever beer bottles, ashtrays, guitar picks, records, milk cartons, paperbacks, a stack of waterlogged notebooks...and the reason that I liked M was because I could tell that he was still afraid of what can be lost rather than won, and because, in his own kind of pathetic way, he rejected the bullshit in other people, even if he had a bullshit of his own, and because he still believed that life could coexist with the spiritual death of Bohemian Brooklyn, and because he didn't at the same time, and because when we got scared we didn't leave each other, we only threatened to, and because we made love and sang and painted and wrote and did lots of other pointless things.

I might have mentioned La Rondine in a letter to Lena actually—I compared La Rondine to a dream I had of Lena—or maybe it was the other way around; I suggested that maybe Lena was La Rondine—a poem I wrote, a song I hummed to myself.

And La Rondine doesn't know about Lena either, how we say things to each other like *Je t'aime bien* and *te quiero* and the objective, almost artful way we make love. Desire and betrayal—betrayal and a functional absence of resolution. And between the two of them, La Rondine's letters[51] are the most like she really is: lyrical, and incoherent, and charming, and terribly sad.

I imagine that she has moved to Berlin and stays up late at night in the winter—wearing mens sweaters, drinking whiskey straight from the bottle, making love to men and women at different times—whenever she wants to.

I imagine that she drinks coffee at bohemian cafés—that she talks about technological futures and poetry and film and authenticity and sex. (This is romanticized.)

(But this also is my unfading epiphany[52]—this distance that keeps approaching nearness.)

---

51 It's so difficult writing you M. I don't know exactly, but I gave you a reason in my last letter. I feel incomplete, crude, shapeless, not able to catch my best self. You embody Poetry, Beauty, Utopia: you're so far, so unreal. I'm afraid of not being enough...not in respect to you, but to myself. And so, sometimes, I think again to the words you told me while we embraced during that long, incredibly short! night. I constantly feel words slipping away from my mouth. Your lips: soft and alive, penciled with sharp bird wing paintbrush. Fruit skin without pulp. Your skin: polished and sweet and brushed with honey. Questions are becoming impossible to ignore, and the world is so...terribly wide...afraid of my own freedom. And I tell myself how much I belong to Poetry, Beauty. Solipsism. I'm full of everything (university, theatre, contemporary dance) but nothing seems to be enough. How can my mind, my spirit be so greedy. I find peace just in the little space between two verses. I have my home settled in the wave enjambment. And I hate men, I hate you all. I love you all.

52 A face mutilated: literature did this—eyes covered, face closed. Light bounces off the center of the immediate past.

I shouldn't have torn up the photograph because it was my only one—but at the same time, I was tired of using it like a talisman to ward off unhappiness.

(Memory is an analogy anyway—but what is it an analogy for?)

She is drawn to a point, red and wavering, against the black of vision, naked and beautiful, smoking before the window and the shattered moon.

In the courtyard there are musicians and philosophers and poets who drink among hanging flowers, purple crocuses, and opening geraniums, and in the waning moonlight they hold a discourse on love that doesn't exist in time, and never has.

Lena feels as if life sprang from her fingertips: the fragments of geranium buds—the stars hanging from the courtyard walls.

She does not recall the names of the people assembled in the courtyard; the people who stay up all night discussing love— they are like memories right before disintegration, when all that remains is an obscure shape; a distant sound.

They are like cubist paintings hanging on the fringes of her consciousness; indistinct balls of firey gas, burning at the end of space—glimpses of ideas that have slipped through the net of time and fallen into the little courtyard outside her window...

She is wearing a white cotton dress, smoking cigarettes in her windowsill, flicking ash on whomever walks below her window.

I can only describe her second hand: geranium petals and butterfly wings: the smell of the grass at midnight.[53]

> *Fingers like spiderwebs and stars:*
> *I have felt it all, I have lived through her, like a shadow.*
> We make this up together—we make it true.[54]

53 "I shudder with your touch, I am extended into nature, my veins are the roots of trees, I am swollen with rain, it is the end of spring, I am almost ready to be plucked and washed and eaten under the shade of a tree. (And will we never sleep?) I gasp, I break the surface of the water."

54 But my body was like a harp and her words and gestures were like fingers running upon the wires.

Let's say it was easy for Lena to find men online who were willing to pay for sex.

And that she rarely sold paintings...and that she loved to gossip.

That she loved flowers. That she loved the ballet. That she liked to paint in the style of early Picasso—harlequins with colorful faces.

Lena would knock on my door and talk to me for four or five hours and then leave without warning; New York didn't have an avant-garde she claimed—*she was the avant-garde.*

She liked money; she was famous for two reasons and one of them was good.

She had nicknames that sounded like towns in southern Spain—and she probably made most of those nicknames up herself.

"Lena, let the ocean inherit your paper millions; stay under under my skin; wear white at sunset"—these were things I tried to say to her—but she wanted to paint until the sun came up; and she wanted relentless contact (even if that required illusion and therefore degradation)—and she wasn't the only one, by the way.

She wrote poems to me on the cut up pieces of dresses that she no longer wanted to wear. She started to paint even red flowers blue—she said it was easier to convert the entire world into a single shade than to love its maddening complexity.

I have a picture of her lying on a beach on the roof of my apartment—naked, with a copy of *Les fleurs du mals* on her chest—it's an absurd but predictable image.

And we wanted to give up, Lena and I—we wanted to prostrate ourselves before a harrying, lustful, magic god...Lena: cypress, laurel, palm—a real Greek—a real dancing girl at a grand hotel; stem too slender, top too loose and heavy—Lena.

And I was tired of romantic poems—I told her I wanted true distinction in an obsolete style; cornice or spandrel and god knows what else.

(Lena was abstract.)

She was famous for her fucking and her painting—and I can't think of two better things to be famous for.

She decided she would call me Novalis—said I should write a book called *The Bluest Flower*. She wanted to float along a great, relaxed curve of time. Pleasure wasn't anything for her though—it was only the beginning.

"A writer who can't create pain can't create characters," she told me.

Her rose was extracted from its sheath, placed above the graves of the metaphysically exhausted and the ladder I was building up to the moon was revealed to be made more of water than of stone.

53

New York is like my relationship with Lena: tenderness and life and love and literature, all mixed up with sterility, coldness, and loneliness, so that one doesn't know which is which—it's like pouring salt and pepper out on a grey table and trying to sort out all the grains—putting salt with salt, pepper with pepper.

New York is like the afternoon I spent alone yesterday drinking tea and reading Joanna's letter over and over;—thinking that maybe if I could understand the letter, then I could understand Joanna, and if I could understand Joanna, I could understand the whole world, or at least the interesting parts of it…

Relationships dissolve here like drops of oil in the sea, people use themselves up like tissues at a sappy film, and yes—sex should be a perpetual twilight—but it's only really for people interested in annihilation.

I told Lena last night that she reminded me of La Rondine, and even though it was true, it was an incredibly stupid thing to say—but Lena has to understand that I'm trying to recover something—not just a word—a sea, a rising fire.

And I'm awful at it, I know—I'm very bad at recovering the things I've lost.

I am soaked by tonight's freezing rain.

The radiators won't come on; neither will the lights.[55]

---

55 "…flowers, it's flowers…I think…" Ellebelle said, still trailing off from her last trail-off. "You know Renoir. He." Belmonte's cigarette drags had become increasingly contemptuous. "Why don't you think before you open your mouth Ellebelle?" Belmonte said, looking directly into her eyes. "I'm not saying the bar for discussion here is particularly high, but even if you don't count some of the things that M says, or Herzen's most caustic comments, you are really a hell of a disgrace." Ellebelle looked at Wallace. Wallace looked at M. M had left without anyone noticing; it was so hard to see with just a few candles going.

Then I became scattered, I got on a plane, left Milan in a hurry—scattered like a scent, a petal fallen halfway off a lemon tree in Brooklyn...

Brooklyn: where people talk about nothing. Dance in Prospect Park and smoke cigarettes to keep the time. Take the train to Bedford Avenue to watch beautiful people speak dialects of embarrassed intimacy. Buy critical theory books and expensive jewelry. Become actors after seeing Shakespeare in the Park. Become directors after someone shows *Cries and Whispers* on a rooftop projector.

Where Lena sells her paintings to rich men who she lets into bed with her (Lena says it is a custom as old as lying itself).

Where Lena sends home money to her parents. Where Lena becomes who she wants to become—and where she doesn't.

Where Lena intercepts my letters from La Rondine and tears them into paper swans. Where Lena cries: "Stay with me... stay with me..."

Where Lena extends across the surface of my whole body—like a shadow city built on the exact topology of the original.

Where Lena drifts away in fragments...where Lena is embedded in my consciousness like a piece of obsidian in a flower bed...

(Lena—that bleak, empty emotion...)

Where art is our private language, where love is our private hope—where love is the conflict of detail that constitutes our emotional vulnerability.

Where I am suspended in the web of a definite unwavering present—which is like being on a train perpetually leaving the station of a place I don't want to leave.

Where I'm seeking a single principal to tether myself to—something that can bring a mind to a focus—like a single speck of light—

Where all the only details are expressionistic:

lust, tendresse, hatred, love, das Ding…jazz, tango, La Rondine, Magdalena, Claire's knee, The Recognitions, pataphysics, critical theory, Days of Heaven, Potato Head Blues, modern architecture, narcissism, fleeting youth…

Where categories only create more categories. Where lovers only create more lovers.

Where the release always depends on instants. Where instants always depend on faith.[56]

---

56 "M, I want to peel away the light of stars like onion skins until I reach the core which is the very stuff of light…"

Musil, Döblin, Hesse wrote from the rim of the abyss. And that is commendable, since almost nobody wagers to write from there. But Kafka writes from out of the abyss itself. To be more precise: as he's falling. When I finally understood that those had been the stakes, I began to read Kafka from a different perspective. Now I can read him with a certain composure and even laugh thereby. Though no one with a book by Kafka in his hands can remain composed for very long.

But in general, what comes out of the dreams are the fragments of references—that is, my subconscious is in the process of working through a story, so when I am dreaming, it's being written from inside there.

And look: something is always lost in the mirror of the ethical just as something is always lost in the mirror of cinema—just as something is lost in the mirror of the other.

The synthetic art is really the art that acts as the sun which secretly gives the moon its light. The synthetic art is the one that you make out of your dreams. That dream is whatever you want it to be: it can be a song or it can be the simple awareness that one is not awake.[57]

So when I say that I begin anywhere, it's because I don't know what, at that point, is to be the beginning or the end. When I start to write, that's the beginning. I haven't decided that the story has to start like that; it simply starts there and it continues, and very often I have no clear idea about the ending—I don't know what's going to happen. It's only gradually, as the story goes on, that things become clearer and abruptly I see the ending...

57 (La Rondine is a film I played in my head. Lena is a film I wrote for La Rondine to watch.)

Because every modern novel has two characters a phoney and a hero and the hero inevitably reveals the phoney to be what he is and you (the reader) can't detect anywhere that subtle difference between people who are real and those who aren't, because while you'd like to be Hamlet (genius/hero/comedian/tragedian/murderer) you always end up playing Claudius (murderer/usurper/fraud) instead.

But people are all the usurpers of themselves, so you just have to pray that you don't meet your own black prince one day—though one day, you always do.

Music goes beyond all that, of course, but what I mean specifically is that Mahler—his music and his language and the ways the two bundle our emotions into something extraneous and fold them back into the single over-overwhelming emotion called "symphony"—represents the images I see when I fall asleep: sesame and lilies, bathwater and the color yellow; Lena and La Rondine, Chekhov and Stanislavsky, Alice and her guitar, Wallace and Ellebelle, Jove and Belmonte, and Herzen and his poems, my sister in Dresden, Lena crying like a child...

Some other things that Mahler represents:
how I feel about dying (unsure)
how I feel about sex (sure)
how I feel about love (how I feel about literature)
how I feel about literature (how I feel about dying)

What it amounts to is that I insist on the unheard of idea that man was meant for something else—and if you've never seen Woody Allen's *Stardust Memories*, you should see it—if just for the last scene, which is endlessly beautiful—but I'm bad at describing the things I love, I think.

Kafka's frozen sea: heaving.

The freedom of music being an existential necessity.

But you don't have to write music, or shoot a film even, to have access to the inner-lightness of art—it's there for us, waiting, like a logical proof or a Nabakov butterfly or one of those cello suites by Bach; or like a trumpet like an aria—Ellington's hands on the record, slashing open a miracle of silence.

Jove says the solos are tucked into something incredibly uninteresting, so that they always catch him by surprise—

And look at how each individual person is like their own complex weather system: unaware of the vast operatic chaos of human bullshit—look how a feather can fuck up the whole system as it floats down from the carcass of a bird struck in midair by a propeller plane.

And listen to how Satchmo can swipe beautifully across a number like an evening across the sky.

And just for reference, none of my days in Brooklyn ever work out: time surges up, plucks down the structures of being here; women improvise their own music; dance up and down the shore—what no one wants is to be told how to move or how to give faith to someone who can actually receive it like a gift...

And there could be quietude instead of longing.

There could be someone else, but I don't know who she could be.

It's time for Jelly Roll. (That's what Jove says.)

We'll say, somewhat miraculously, that it was a blue flower.

I took the bus to Pennsylvania. I went home-home. Lena cried for fifteen minutes because she couldn't understand why I was leaving.

"I need a break."

"A break from what?"

"A break from everything. "

"What's everything? "

No answer...

And I couldn't explain—I can never explain anything clearly—that I wanted to be purified—that we needed the courage to be honest—to see simple things and state them simply.

And that we needed to be apart; that that's why I was going home—

And because I wanted to sit in my parents' garden and read; because I wanted to drink fresh milk and eat simply and sleep like a dog in the sun; because the soul becomes part of its environment—because our environs integrate with us; because the soul is rich and alive, like soil ten feet deep...

And because I wanted to learn how to love again—and because I want to relearn forgotten knowledge; and because I wanted to write again—like I used to—because I wanted to feel like a mariner adrift in the Aegean, looking up at the constellations...

A clasp of sound, a plate broken on the floor, a speaking world turning me out of doors—trying to make me understand...

The kitchen in the darkness.

The misery of love.

"This is for all the time I spent obsessively wrapped around you, M, chain-smoking— all of your books piled around us—dressed like a courtesan, or something ridiculous—wishing you'd really notice me," Lena was saying on her way out.

"Lena—what are you talking about?" M asked.

"I'm talking about the note you left under my door this morning—"[58]

"I thought you liked my notes—"

"Well they're always so fantastically pretty that I can't actually believe that I inspired them."

"Lena—"

"M, why do you treat me like I'm stupid?"

"I don't—"

"Of course you do, silly—"

"I treat you like yourself—that's it—"

"Well maybe that's the problem."

Lena took a step down the hallway.

"Where the hell—?"

"I'm not really leaving you M, because you're going to leave me, remember?"

"Who said that?"

"You're just going to, I know it—"

"Even clearest emotions have dimensionality—four to be factual about it—because everyone who has any sense knows

---

58 Of all the notes that M ever taped to his door for Lena, the only one she ever kept was the first: *Lena—the ecosystem of the soul is ridiculously delicate: the slightest error in its variables leads to chaos and magical, terrifying fluctuations of possibility. Your legs go limp, you fall to your knees. Your nerves are trying to mend themselves—but they always end up in knots. (And so my nerves always end up in knots just like yours do.) And no one, including the impersonators hired to replace us, can comment on how it is that we arrived at a place beyond dying or love…because nothing is ever symbolic Lena, for instance, how your decaying mouth keeps begging for water, and how I pour it over your lips because I am weak, and you are thirsty. And how everything in the universe (including roses) is searching, but not for itself.*

that music is the fourth dimension," M said, turning around and walking over to the record player.

"Oh, don't hide behind one of your beloved 'Three B's'."

"I don't hide behind them—I hide through them—"

Lena shook her head:

"I grew up near the beach, M—I don't know if you really know anything about my childhood—anyway—I remember speaking to my grandfather in Spanish, and walking through mango groves talking to the birds about my dreams. Everything was made of rain. The sea, the clouds. The stars, too, must have be made of rain—if they were made of anything—M are you listening?"

"Schubert's name doesn't begin with 'B'—and he's probably the most important of my escape-artists."

"You aren't listening—"

"Of course I'm listening—I'm a chronic listener."

"Well you don't show it."

"I don't like being obvious."

Lena bit her lip:

"Let's cut time across the throat—let's watch the years stain the carpet red—because once you leave me M, things will start going by so fast—"

"Things are always going by so fast."

"Well then why aren't you chasing after me?"

"Because like you said Lena—and this is honestly a terrible shame—you'll end up chasing after me."

"Because you're in love with somebody else—"

"Essentially."

"It's like we're living in a condemned house with a roof that's about to fall in," Lena said.

"Isn't it wonderful?—pressing the evening like a sliver of glass against the heart? spending all day in the rain? waiting for a single face to identify itself with the divine—and finding it—?"

M said, lifting *Der Tod und das Mädchen* onto the record player.

"You're being oblique—"

"What I'm talking about, really, is the polyphonic lyric of the everyday..."

"M..."

"You should have seen me in Washington Square yesterday—the sun came out in the evening after the storm had passed—and I was really in a mood—it's hard to explain, but..."

"Let me guess, you had some experience of real innocence and realized how fucked-up our being together is?—is that it?"

Lena had begun to tear up.

M returned to the doorway, the music playing softly behind him.

"In short, being a Chekhovian means having the decency to extract the sweetness from life before it turns to chalk dust and silence—that's all I'm trying to say."

"But things are fucked up, with us—aren't they?—can you just admit that?"

"I already have," M said.

No, it didn't matter, because they could listen to *Trois Gymnopédies* over and over until they fell asleep.

Music used to be a flower of silence blooming on a snowy plain, M told her once, that was what Bach was, at least.

And it was always better to fuck to Bach, they agreed, than Beethoven, and it was better to fuck to Schubert above all: because the inner tension of pathos could only be communicated by harmony, not gestures.

And Lena was as obedient as a sheep, and cried with joy when he moved inside of her, and she would tug his shoulders towards her as if she was trying to have him reach some ultimate depth that neither of them could fully fathom.

Only after someone had left him, would M begin to understand how much their existence together had been a miracle. How skin and sweat always revealed a sunken world; how the moon over the Brooklyn skyline looked like an unfurled magnolia.

BWV 1044 on record.

Lena puts a hand to her lips and smiles slightly. The courtyard is empty, the sun races across the grass.

She lets a shawl fall from her shoulders because it's growing warmer, the night chill dissipating. Softly she hears a woman singing. It is still morning.

Time curves, and the love she feels is as deep as life: the crocuses opening on the window, the taste of burnt coffee on her tongue; paintings of purple flowers; purple petals crushed between her fingers.

(Flowers to make medicine out of.)

She knows that her lungs are giving out, but that there is no death here.

And she hopes that it rains. She wants to hear the great thunderclap of the divine. Her nostrils flare. She strokes her flanks with her hands, rough like the hands of all painters.

(And she is lucent blue: like all imagined beings.)

Love will make us real.

We've been parted at the breastbone, she and I. (She into the tunnel of a book, disappearing.)

Forget-me-not flowers, fire-robed goddess.

These are our carnations; flowers out of time.

There is a ghostly demarcation—what I call myself stands out as a line that cannot be crossed; my dreamlike innerlife.

I know that it's important to give up on myth, heroism, love—on a search for literal truth beginning with the unliteral Word—but my impulse is to give up or give in, always; to swerve sideways into the chastisement of friends and lovers and everyone else in New York who gives a damn, or doesn't.

Is this going too far?—certain secular truths, certain secular vessels are begging us, like cheap whores, to be broken after being loved.

As Lena said, "The soul is a flowerpot, but the roots grow in the air."[59]

I don't know what she meant, but at the same time I do— balance occurs when limits are transcended. When we are limited, we are out of balance—*c'est mauvais*—so we must grow in the air, grow through the air, down to the ground of our being.

We spend whole evenings, whole nights talking nonsense. We practice Zen to test the firmness of a good or bad fuck. Lena says that my lips taste like day old bread. Lena laughs and goes out to the fire-escape, where I can see her from the bed.

She talks to cicadas—the moon, she says, is an elastic fetter.

59   And it really was true about Lena that everything Beethoven could do in a symphony or Proust in 3,300 pages, she could do in a split second or less with a glance or biting of the lower lip—which was why she had so many lovers and why so many of them ended up more lonely than even M after she inevitably disappeared: because she opened something up in people that began like a dream, but ended up like something more real than anything that ever happened in dreams. She said that she just wanted to die free of everything—of painting, of men and women, of love; that she wanted to die free even of death (which was impossible but something she wanted die free from anyway—despite the paradox). Lena told M that she'd had her first gallery show when she was ten and that she used to show off for adults by drawing with both hands at once like Leonardo and that she taught herself five or six languages as a child and that her favorite was Portuguese because she said it sounded like she felt—whatever that was. (Once, she told M that she had read Aristotle's *Organon* in Greek—three times start to finish—and that she had come to realize that the law of the excluded middle was bullshit, and that if M had nine or ten hours or so to listen, she could explain it to him.)

63

Alice let him do whatever he wanted; he let her do what she wanted—and only when they'd talk afterwards (never before), would they let themselves appear meaningful to each other.

They talked about the concrete elements of the places they grew up: the houses, the sounds, the smells. The gradations of light and the different pitches that thunder could reach depending on the time of year and how scary it was when it boomed.

They talked about how much they loved their parents, and how strange it was when they got old enough to resent their parents for the values they had chosen for their children.

They talked with the windows open and the neighborhood kids playing outside until God knows what time—it was hard not to talk about things like that for hours (they hardly even felt the time passing)—

Sometimes they'd go out on his fire escape to listen to the crickets—which were pretty paltry in Brooklyn in the summer—but they were nice to listen to anyway, the crickets—even though they made M think painfully and consciously of Lena.

Alice liked watching the cat slip in and out of the door when she made love to M. She liked walking around in her underwear and how he looked at her body in the mirror she had hung on the wall.

And straightaway she had known love was dangerous.

She knew it by the time that she was fourteen: she knew it all the time—and she knew it all over again when she met M.

"M, don't you just want to be able to float into the ether sometimes, the ether that lives behind the moon?"

"Lena…"

"Yes you idiot, I'm being ridiculous, and if I wasn't here you'd be milling around Williamsburg, eating yogurt, and trying to pick up seventeen-year-old models who just want someone to love them for who they are on the inside."

"That doesn't sound so bad—"[60]

"Well it should."

"Lena, the only thing that sounds bad to me right now, is sleeping alone—so can you please just come back to bed?"

"I'd rather sit in the window and watch you look lonely—"

"In the old days I could have slept easily, and you could have done whatever it is you do, tell the future by the progress of the moon from the fire-escape, read tarot cards to the neighbor's cat…but now I'm too fragile—I've become like an old man."

"Go meet a nameless girl on the subway, like you know you want to M."

"Wide eyes, nice teeth—presto—"

"Let me finish my cigarette, then we can sleep, ok?—poor little boy."

"Now your breath will taste like tobacco—"

"You like the taste of cigarettes."

"That's true, I didn't say it was a bad thing."

"Why don't you ever tell me what you think about on the nights you can't sleep?"

"Because I'm trying to gain some distance from my own nostalgia, Lena—"

"I hope you put it all down in a terrible little poem one day, just for me—your nostalgia—"

60 M was thinking of the last scene in *La Dolce Vita*.

"Of course I will."

Lena put her cigarette out on the fire-escape, slid down from the windowsill, and made it back into bed in two steps, falling asleep as soon as her head hit the pillow, which was instantly.

What he called his novel was a big notebook culled from from dozens of smaller notebooks (with scissors and glue) that was beginning to resemble a dadaist bible.

He told Jove privately that the novel would never be published; it hastened on toward a thousand pages and he only had a dim sense of what he was doing—like with Musil and his man without qualities, except not as good.

The elation of bullshit, he called it: *the bullshit of elation.*

When he was working, Lena would get so desperate for attention, that she would lay on the floor, smoking, listening to record after record, staring at the ceiling, acting like she didn't want any attention at all; contemplating the spectral conditions of their relationship—waiting for a wave of desire to pick him up from the typewriter and carry him to her on the floor, or off to bed.

She was a symbolist music; a paradise of intoxicating cheap perfumes and fresh mint ground between her teeth; the shredded remains of the postmodern Marsyas she would paint over herself when nobody was looking—the blues of Bechet and Bix Beiderbecke—the erotic violet of Gauguin movingly interjected into the green flora of a tulip garden.

He wrote his novel to impress Lena; to remember her; to forget her—which was why he was writing it about somebody else; he was like Thales, he thought, trying to explain the weather without mythology—trying to explain ultimate substance, change, the existence of the world—Lena, La Rondine—a tangerine half peeled on the floor.

Herzen fucking Ellebelle; Ellebelle wrapping her small arms around his thick chest—the thought made Wallace's throat constrict, and he let out a "Fuck!" under his breath. What were they doing outside for so long? It was *just* a cigarette anyway.

It was terrible to live with a woman who wouldn't care for you the way you cared for her, Wallace realized.

And Wallace was tired of being the merely plausible guy.[61] The guy you'd never commit any serious spiritual junk to...and Herzen was such an asshole coming in here, eating his Chinese food—the noodles, the lo-mein, the fried rice, the chicken, the pork, everything covered in the sweet-and-sour sauce that came in those little plastic packets, mixed together indistinguishably on the plate, swallowed down with mouthfuls of warm beer—reading his poems, talking to M about books no one else had read—putting his hand on Ellebelle's thigh while everyone was drinking coffee and talking, generally not giving a shit about what Wallace would think.

Wallace put on a recording of Bechet's *Lonesome Blues*.

Herzen and Ellebelle came back in with Cheshire cat grins on their faces.

The mixture of literature, art, Chinese food, coffee, and erotic competition was so thick in the air that if M had stuck around, Herzen thought, he would have gagged, not simply because Chinese food made him sick—but because he was averse to all combinations of three or more smells.

"Where did M go? I need to give him something," Herzen asked.

61 M watched them sitting together and thought about how metaphysical speculation only reinforced his way of perceiving the world: physical beauty could break your heart with its fragility, or under the guise of summer and nights that never ended until the sun rose. The spiritual truth of Brooklyn was that it existed, that no other place existed like it, except the thousand other places it had borrowed its lifestyle from. Couples were the same everywhere: they fucked the same, they hated the same, they made up the same...the music was making him feeling rosy and romantic. What time was it anyway?

"What do you want to give him?"

"A book."

"What book?" Wallace asked.

"A book about women getting killed in Mexico and a great novelist with an unknown identity. And other things."

"Sounds rad."

Herzen shook his head.

"'Pretending that I was dedicated to a profound existence while all the time I barely dipped my toe into the terrible waters of feeling.' You know what that means?—it means you don't know if it's cool or not, Wallace."

"*Yo*—maybe I'll read it. I read that Gaddis book after you gave it to me—"

"That's mostly true—but did you entropize? Entropize yourself through the book Wallace?"

"I don't know what you're talking about dude."

"I'm asking if you developed entropy-sickness, like malaria? From the Gaddis..."

"Dude, *come on.*"

Herzen shrugged, choosing not to respond. Wallace, annoyed, went into his room to play guitar.

Ellebelle, who had taken a seat on the futon, looked at Herzen sympathetically, and smiled.

When Wallace was out of earshot, Herzen looked at Ellebelle, and blew smoke into her face.

"That guy sucks."

Ellebelle shook her head.

"I love him Herzen."

"Yeah, but he sucks."

"You're just jealous, you big lug—"

Ellebelle gave Herzen a kiss on the cheek.

She was wearing[62] a sweater vest and skirt which made her look like a schoolgirl, right down to the cigarette, and the thinly veiled desire for experience.

"You're sweet Herzen, but you're a terrible friend."

"You two can go fuck yourselves—" Herzen said, "I'm gonna go find M—"

Herzen thought of half-choking Ellebelle in the dark; cumming as she pushed him away, before pulling him closer as the rudeness rushed out from him...he imagined slipping his finger just inside her anus, pushing her face into the pillow, flipping her over like a used book...he thought of kissing her on the forehead, slapping her across the face, biting into her neck. He imagined the sound of her voice as she whispered in his ear; the sound of her voice sobbing with the joy of completion in his arms...

Pauvre Wallace.[63]

62   "Who wants more beer?" Herzen asked. "Can we get back to Croce for a second..." "Can we stick with Cézanne for a second Belmonte?" "Anyone want more ice cream? There's still a lot left and you know I can't eat it all myself," Wallace said happily. "I'm sorry I think I'll pass," Belmonte said. "Me too," M added. "Pasteurized milk makes me sick." Ellebelle stood up, smoothing her polka dot skirt over her supple, pale thighs; sighing slightly but erotically, looking at Herzen. "Well I'll have another beer..." she said. "No ice-cream though." "Did someone say something about Kant before?" M asked. "I thought someone did?" "No one said anything about Kant," Belmonte huffed, forgetting that he had brought Kant up a few minutes before.

63   Somewhere, M guessed, Kierkegaard says everything about this sort of thing: the parks filled with the bourgeoisie: the impossibility of faith: the total blank of other people...that faith meant anguish and anguish meant faith: that the more and more you pluck at the flower of the microcosm, the more you realize that you're staring at the mouth of an archangel, about to swallow you whole.

O

"*When I give the commonplace a higher meaning, the known the dignity of the unknown, the finite the illusion of the infinite, I romanticize it.*"

-Novalis, *Fragment 105*

pening scene:

M wanders through Grand Central Station with binoculars. It is winter. He is wearing a peacoat. The scene shifts to London: a woman writes a letter on the tube. She is romantic looking: wild hair, a colorful raincoat, a purse full of books. It is also winter in London. The people on the train look unhappy.

The scene shifts again: M receives a letter from the woman on the train. It explains a way to find her through time. The letter says: "*I am not the one you are looking for, but here is how to find me in case I am.*"

The scene shifts again: the London woman goes to a screening of *Stardust Memories*. She is wearing the same colorful raincoat.

The scene shifts again: M is scaling the walls of Grand Central Station. An old lady screams. Children point.

M begins to fall.

(I don't know what happens next.)

you once said that you could do anything you wanted with words and if i have any sort of reciprocal skill it's with psychology and consequently my relationships are synthetic adhesions of dependence and repulsion and so it seems inevitable yes and yes perhaps important but what you really have to recognize is that that Unknown that you're talking about has everything to do with our natures and the way that the forces at play in this whole interchange (your contact my response thesis anthesis and everything after) are exactly those prenaturally uncanny gifts that we've both fortunately/unfortunately been given and because of this it's clear isn't it? that we found each other to help destroy each other and i've known this all along and you've fended off my observation too the whole time (each of us playing our role) because as george steiner says psychoanalysis is really just applied linguistics in which case we are both shivas to one another inhabiting and destroying each other at the point of contact and destruction is really assured and who can say how much of this is literally true and how much is simply uncomfortably close (and i've tested this theory before in parts haven't i?) but the point is that as long as i can train my sights close enough to your foxhole you'll keep your head down but at the same time you keep using mirrors joanna to get a glance above ground because for a long time you've been considering either sticking your head up or just waving a white flag and advancing towards my superior strategic position and yes again here we are talking about it (the Unknown) the no man's land in the middle and we need a christmas truce (i've proposed vienna or a phone call or anything really) and don't think for a second i don't know that my strategic position really is superior (it's germany after the marne halfway into france but doomed by my own inability to reach paris before winter) and it's all so bloody literal and abstract at the same time isn't it? (you and i) the way metaphors spin between us like whirligigs out of an initially simple thought (the basic notion that we've always known each other that we've been sending messages into voids forever and that the recognitions was a wormhole a rent in space/time through which to receive those messages and that's not a simple notion at all is it? no it's not it's wonderfully romantic-metaphysical but it's the point i've got to make it's the point i've been working my way to this the whole time: SOS).

The radiator on. The teapot whistling on the gas stove. What is she thinking about, laying there?—a lover perhaps; someone she let kiss her in the doorway the night before— someone whom she let fuck her right there on the floor—the floor on which she's lying all alone now, thinking about her life and her painting—how it keeps her alive, just the possibility of it—the potential to breathe through it (the painting).

Because when it's happening, she can't think about anything else, because it becomes like dying—that feeling of loving and losing—

And how precious it is to her: this magnificent emotion roiling in her chest, like the water in the radiator pipes, slipping up to her brain and mixing with the voice that cries "death, death, death" to produce steam.

And it's always been death which she has to resist—death: so lovely, and so horrifying, and so musical and alive.

Lena has rich oily skin and hair, which she washes with lavender and thyme oil. She runs her hand through it now.

Later maybe, after she pours the hot water from the kettle into the pot, she'll lay back down and cry and laugh to herself— thinking that she can't afford to rent a studio in Williamsburg— that she can't afford anything that costs money in New York.

These moments[59] are inexhaustible to her; each one of them is unique and perfect.

---

59 From *Platonic Excursions*: "The past significantly, is closed; that is to say: our re-experience of it is not an experience of the original phenomenon, it is a derivation of that phenomenon. Memories are not real (if by real we mean immediate sensory experience). The vividness of the original phenomenon is not matched by the re-experience. Remembering an original phenomenon over time is like drinking a cup of hot soup: each spoonful diminishes in total heat. The objects of past experience do not persist with our memories; we may remember a face or a building or a painting that over the course of our lives ceases to exist, and this creates a haunting dissonance between the subjective reality of our memory and the reality of things outside of us."

It begins to snow.

The tea-kettle whistles.

She rolls on her belly and pushes herself up and slinks over to the stove—pouring the hot water from the kettle into the teapot, the dark leaves already scattered on the bottom...

She adds milk and just a little bit of honey.

70

And look at how happy the cat is drinking his milk.

And listen to how happy the kids sound playing in the street outside. Look how happy M is as he strokes my hair back over my eyes and kisses me on the neck. People are happy because they are here and nowhere else. Because the earth, this fucked up, violated, polluted, violent planet has put people on it to be happy, and not to close themselves off to whatever good things are still left, whatever those things are.

I'm not in mourning because I'm in love with death, but because I'm in love with a life that is always dying around me.

M is obsessed by what he loses over time, but I'm obsessed by what I gain:

How a person arrives with a full knowledge of each particle of the universe, how each of us moves through the other, how a sea-liner falls off the edge of the world, how a wastebasket is filled with roses, how with different hands I could write in more variant, more gorgeous inks...how with four colors I could have at least four hands painting the sky.

Elsewhere old men live with grief for the lives they have wasted in order to gain wealth and power.

Elsewhere, old women dance naked holding the dugs of their breasts in their hands, still heavy with birth-milk.

I go to M: I offer him my open/closed body.
I mask myself.
"Thanks for the show," he says.

We talk about making films together, Lena and I—but then again—here she is, crying while I wait for the bus out of New York.[60] We pour through each other like streams of water. We touch, we move away again—but we don't have any good reason for why we are the way we are; we are afraid of living maybe—afraid of being alone, afraid of giving each other pleasure—and pleasure is a part of it—but at the same time, both of us are terrified by pleasure like we're terrified by thunderstorms (and we're terrified by thunderstorms).

We need nature—both of us—we need plant life creeping up around us, pulling us down with strong hands under the soil; demystifying the world—carrying us into the strange darkness of human love.

Lena opening the fridge, asking who ate all the eggs. Lena going out onto the fire escape to talk to Jove about Egyptian gods. Lena pacing around, laughing at one of Belmonte's extremely odd jokes. Lena writing a novel in pictures. Lena drawing over Wallace's record covers when he isn't looking.

Lena and I combing the entire apartment looking for an ax; Lena and I skating on the ice all morning.

Lena and I—something that isn't there anymore because all of a sudden I'm with La Rondine, our feet dangling over La Seine—and I've gone back in time—took Dante's spiral stairs up to the floor of heaven...

A last reflecting pool: a basin to pool transitional images; homesickness and bohemian poverty—one after the other—

60 I like Brooklyn even though I hate it too: how everyone's forgotten how to cleave ethics from aesthetics, or how to find the elegance of life in the inelegance, or how to tell someone that you don't really love them and that you just liked the way their lips formed a halo around a cigarette or a winebottle or your cock. This makes sense to me, anyway: screwing in the dark, not whispering anything but dirty words and secrets, doing laundry together, carrying those big trash bags full of clothing five blocks in the heat, watching Spanish soap operas, waiting for the spin cycle to end...

tapestries of moss growing around the dogwood tree—an apartment on Knickerbocker Avenue with so-so plumbing and the occasional rat under the sink—with films we watch at all hours, with a peculiar despair that breeds itself out of the desire to be desired—with mornings that glow with sunset—

And the more complex things get, the more we need to need to rationalize what it is that we've been doing with our lives; the paperwork multiplies; the intricacies of simple things become more and more impossible—like sitting in bed and watching Lena smoke a cigarette and talk on the phone in Spanish.

And as Jove says, the ocean of life is a puddle we can just step across, or lay our coats down over for a lady in white; and as Dante says—Eros makes and unmakes a person all at once.

And all of this should give me joy—all of *this*—in its *thisness*—whatever that is.[61]

(I know it.)

(As if I could invest my self with inhuman love.)

(As if I, at the edge of a cliff, could stumble backwards towards safety.)

61 Every woman he ever loved had taught him that, that love was something that people experienced with their whole bodies and not just their heads—La Rondine or Lena or Alice (the most important ones)—but even one night stands, or the blow jobs that were like completing a trilogy—had taught him something about the necessity of spiritual embodiment...

Everything: La Rondine, and Paris—kissing by the water; an old woman lighting a cigarette *déjà la journeé aux dicibles désirs*—Alice playing her guitar in the doorway; Alice putting on makeup; Alice listening to music with headphones on; Alice making up one of those perfect lies of hers; Alice just being one of those people—Alice being the one I go to when I feel alone.

Alice just because I can—Alice as an idea; as a girl in the way; as a girl I met in line for a movie; as a girl on her way to nowhere; as the girl I see to make Lena jealous—as a girl I use to cancel out Lena like the other side of an equation.

Alice dearest, Alice darling—Alice who walks around in her underwear to show off for me—who knows she deserves it—that her body deserves it—deserves to be seen. Yes that Alice, the one who lets me read her diaries—*who makes me read her diaries*—and who keeps them out of spite more than anything—and because of the sensual nonsense of being young and staying up late and living in New York and sleeping with men who drive her crazy—men like me—men who sleep with other women; men who are unreliable; men who write poetry.

Alice, so immature, so ambivalent, so eager to always prove that she's older than she is; Alice whom Lena would crush like a paper-plate; Alice who would look up to Lena as a model of aestheticized unreliability, nonsense, and dishonesty; who would conspire with Lena against me if she could—Alice who would try to seduce Lena, just like Lena would try to seduce her. Alice, dear Alice, who records videos of herself reading poetry with a cigarette in her mouth and posts them online for her friends to comment on; Alice who right now doesn't know anything and in a few years will know everything…Alice who read Paracelsus and Max Beerbohm just because she saw them next to my bed; Alice who bought a plane ticket to Berlin that doesn't leave for another year.

Alice who can smell Lena on me from a mile away—Alice who always knows where I've been and where I'm going. Alice who is like this all the time, like crazy—telling me to come along; to jump back into bed; to sing at the top of my lungs; to make up my mind or to get on down the road.

The old woman in the doorway; a Fisher King at the top of the tarot deck; Alice writing a song about me—Alice pretending it's about someone else—Alice not even bothering to change my name...*and the sex*—I mean—it's pornography with her: it's moaning, licking, crying, scratching, sobbing, howling—it's giving up to give in—it's giving in to give up—it's nothing like with Lena; it has none of the tender nobility—and that's the charm of Alice; her secret; her gnosis—my reason for taking the train uptown; for coming in out of the rain just to say hello; for putting up with her long digressions about why I'm not reliable and why, when I'm not around, she feels like cutting all her hair off or calling someone else (someone who actually cares).

Yes to sum it up: the old woman in the doorway, pornography, Alice and her guitar, Alice and the way she mirrors Joanna's letters, Lena's secrets, La Rondine's absence... Alice as the half-step away from from the major tonic (because like I said—coming in out of the train, stopping in for an hour, making love, taking a shower, listening to the guitar...the husky voice; the eyes asking me to look away—to come again, or don't come back[62]).

And her eyes are like something a magician pulls out of a hat—a miracle of diffusion and uncertainty—which is exactly what I need—and we both know it...

62 Alice liked to talk about stars floating above some endless depth; she said we mirrored them, the stars—she said we could hold their light in our hands like poems inside a book. (This is one of the ways she mimicked Lena without knowing it).

So follow the logic like a thread out of a Cretan tunnel—
"tell me what I'm here for"—*"I'm here for you"*—that's what I'm
saying—that's the gesture I'm making—that's what I'm saying
on my way out the door.[63]

63 Sometimes she would just lay on her bed and pull up her skirt and say fuck me, and
sometimes she blindfolded M and told him that she was going to do whatever she wanted.
She liked the feeling of running her fingers along his ribs and abdomen where his body
was strongest. She liked turning those fingers around his back and running them up his
spine and feeling him tense as if he had received a chill. M was feminine. M was like a
piece of wire that she could bend with her fingers and wrists. M was free even though she
could tell that he was somebody else's. They were free together even though they were
both somebody else's in the end. (Who M really belonged to, Alice didn't know.) Alice
often talked about stars drifting over the sea at night. A shore where people waited and
drank and played the fiddle and sang—eyes without light and silence instead of names.
Alice had been sleeping with men since she was fourteen. She knew what she was doing in
bed. She talked about going to New Orleans and a guitar player she fell in love with there,
and M thought that she saw New Orleans the way most people see Paris.

One afternoon when he was too tired and too emotional for a second fuck (meaning he
couldn't get a hard-on again) Alice decided it would be better to go home rather than lay
around languorously, doing nothing, or reading one of his philosophy books...and so not
as a consequence of inaction, but rather, the enchantment of desire—he never saw her
again.

I am making a novel out of the scraps of your breasts, the bits of your hair, the fruit of your thighs, the sweat on your forehead and navel, the nubs of your spine, I can feel all with my hands.

This is the kind of book that a magpie makes out of the thorns and thistles of time. But I cannot really recreate the way you looked at me; the lines are too sharp, too specific—only the dim-coned light remains.

You are nobody. Moans and chants under the moon. Kisses on the nape. Hair that smells like grease and shampoo.

I'm Brando in *Last Tango*—I won't tell you my name, I can't stand names anymore—I'd rather be a grunt...or a shout—but no names.

And now, I feel so close to you—you live in me like a blank lives inside a poem (imageless)—your voice like music without melody; your body like the sun and stars and like the basil plant, flowering in the window.

And like a magpie, I assemble the scraps of you—and you are also like a bird—a swallow—floating along some invisible parabola in space; in and out of time; a parabola that I'm trying to trace backwards.

And the dead come back to life when I think of you—when I summon up the past of that first love we wasted so frivolously. The skin, uncapturable, even with words. Your skin, your lips. The skin of breasts. Skin wet with sweat and saliva. And even Shakespeare could not make skin like you had—even though he could make people otherwise more real than you and I.

I think that New York City is weaned on black milk and grit and dirt and noise, and about how dirty we are on the inside when we cannot love.

Wind whispering to the stars. Nested in the moments of our dying.

Husks of burnt out moons...

But there are other fundamental forces:[64]

I listen to street traffic—watch my friend Charlotte drink her glass of lemonade—listen to her talk about the death of her father; listen to her avoid saying how much she's in pain—

A Knight rapidly jumps f3, c3, f6, c6 at the table one over from ours—Charlotte hardly notices and I don't blame her: the opening sequence of a game of chess is just like any overture (think *Tristan und Isolde*)—so gorgeous you forget it the minute it's over.

Charlotte tells me about how her father demanded a beer the morning he died; how his feet swelled; how he suddenly understood very clearly what was happening to him and how he accepted it with grace—and how death swept over the house she grew up in like a hail storm; how it cleared the power lines; how it felled the trees.

Charlotte has black hair and oval eyes and she says her ancestors must have been gypsies—she wears her hair piled on top of her head and has these big glasses that always seem like they're going to slide right down off the bridge of her nose.

Next to us, a Sicilian Defense is beginning to put itself back

64 "How can a philosophy of love speak about itself? Uncover itself? Philosophy is the rationalizing of experience; or what has sometimes been called phenomenology. But love is irrational, so there can be no philosophy of love...yet philosophy is in the oldest sense, the love of wisdom. Philosophy is itself an embodiment of love. To love, therefore is to philosophize and to philosophize is to love. Socrates understood that philosophy is not dogmatic, fixed, empirical, or academic. It is the extension of the life of the individual into the life of the community. We do philosophy when we become earnest about the possibility for real change through dialogue. This dialogue is not a historical unfolding as Hegel thought, nor is it a result of economic necessity, as Marx thought, but rather, it is the moment that is exchanged between lovers of wisdom: for there to be a true philosophy of love, philosophy must begin to speak about itself. Philosophy therefore, is always subjective, always changing, always local. It is a process, as love is a process. We do not philosophize to reach absolute knowledge, but to become linked to the subtle musical progress of knowledge in the world."

together again out of algebra and habit—Charlotte talks about metaphysical loneliness and I try not to think about La Rondine, or about myself at all, and I try to listen because listening well is a symptom of being good, and because Charlotte has more interesting things to say than I do.

And at the same time—despite myself—I'm thinking of a word that La Rondine always used—*"ebbrezza"*—rapture—a word connected with possession.[65]

So knight to f5, Charlotte—it's our turn now—let's talk about Kierkegaard, knight of faith; let's talk about how we got here; how friendship evolved between us like a spider's web in a windowpane; how each of us is concealing the real tenor of our emotions from the other—and how each moment is like a fractal: divisible into infinitely more intimate expressions of sympathy.

65 (In Greek the word is *mania*, madness. For Plato it was the main path to knowledge. For us it's become the main path to the lunatic asylum.)

It is still light outside at The Hungarian Cafe where Charlotte waits for M at the outdoor tables—having already ordered two black coffees in heavy white mugs—one of which Charlotte has hooked through with her long finger, so that her fingernail clinks on the glass—*tink, tink, tink*—while she waits.

M sits down at the table, unslinging his bag from his shoulder, and smiles at her sheepishly:

"Sorry I'm late."

Charlotte starts to talk about floating over the pale wake of the sea, any sea, until the end of time.

M talks about winters in New York, and the atmosphere of emptiness that settles over the city when it snows.

Laughter: pain: love and so on.

M orders a second coffee. He stirs the coffee with a spoon: a circular motion, repeated—he looks at Charlotte, and he stops.

"When my grandfather was dying, all I remember is no emotion, no sadness even, even though I loved him immensely—" M explains, "there was just a feeling of dread...Christ, I mean I'm probably being redundant saying this to you, but..."

"It's ok M—you don't have to try to understand me— everyone's always trying to understand me, but it doesn't change *it*—" Charlotte says, letting the "*it*" go so that it floats along the surface sheen of her coffee cup like a toy sailboat.

Across the street, M sees someone he doesn't want to see.

Of course the wildness of coffee was always non-fatal, conversations never got so bizarre with nihilism that they actually mimicked it—and this was one of those situations where he wished he smoked French cigarettes—or that he simply knew how to be dishonest.

Death was about being ripped to pieces and stitched together again, he thought—death was about accepting the absence of hope or love or desire[66]—about giving in to the swell, the flutter of the universe as it prophesied its own demise.

Wind—silence—Rilke's poems; the magic of two people not saying anything; the *clink, clink, clink* of Charlotte's nail against the coffee-mug.

And something about Charlotte's expression made M want to lean forward and grasp her hands warmly between his own, but he didn't, and instead, he sank into his seat—drunk on caffeine and presentness and uncertainty.

*

"You know like, when I think about other people dying, the real old people you see buying groceries with their walkers huffing for their last breaths and it's just terrible, I think like: it's just not my turn. It's just not my turn to complain. Same goes with anyone who is not really suffering, I mean physically suffering, in a world of suffering people...am I rambling?"

"No M, you're not rambling—"

"I kinda feel like I've stepped in the puddle of nonbeing, and I'm waiting now for my socks to dry; it's annoying, but all you need is patience and a good radiator...but of course in the

66   He realized that he was not meant to search, not in the active sense of the word—in the sense of waiting—but rather, that he was meant to cultivate a mode of consciousness most appropriate to someone who has lost the will to power.

end it's not a puddle, it's a whole lake—an ocean—an eternity—
you just fall in and you don't realize that's the trick—you don't
realize it because you can't conceive of it—and I don't mean you
Charlotte—I mean everyone..."

"M, what do you think death really *is?*—I don't mean for
you—I mean...on its own, with no one observing it?"

"It's like Zampanò killing the clown in *La Strada*—"

"Be serious—"

"I am being serious, Charlotte—that's the most serious
answer I could have given."

*

They both knew that thinking about death meant enacting
a transcendental violence against the self: that the deep search for
authenticity began with a wave of oceanic sadness.

*

"You always let me do all the talking Charlotte, but you're
the one who really has something to say—"

"Just because I've lost someone I love doesn't mean..."

"No—" M interrupted her, "it does mean something...it
means that the language in you has woken up a little bit—that
everything has woken up a little bit—and that's what death
does—that's what it *should* do to someone...and it *does* mean that
you have something to say to other people..."

Charlotte shook her head sadly.

"You know M, my favorite episode of *La Rayuela* might be
the one where Horacio goes to the concert of Berthe Trépat...
and what does he experience there?—*agape*—and why?—because
people are so obviously fragile and pathetic...and because he has
nothing to win from Berthe Trépat, nothing to take from her,
nothing to prove to her..."

*

"That's part of my thesis actually—" Charlotte said, "the idea that, during trauma, we form all sorts of new connections—that we become like children again—entirely new, entirely plastic—"

They were silent for a few seconds and M took a sip of coffee.

Expression yielded a ripple-shadow: a smile: an identity.

(And who were they?—watching the great stars sweep overhead?)

*

And Charlotte understood what transcendental violence did to someone: it altered them beyond recognition—just like it had altered her father into a resurrection of living silence.

*

"Charlotte, you're like someone living in another dimension, receiving postcards from a metaphysical place."

"Death?"

"Yes, death—of course."

"And are you just a tourist in this dimension?" Charlotte asked.

"Probably," M said.

"But everyone dies—"

"Still—"

"So you think you're a tourist?"

"Probably."

"Why?"

"Because I don't live in the world of death—I live in the false world of life—"

Charlotte smiled again:

"I miss that world, don't take it for granted M."

"You know, sometimes I think about my own life and how shallow it is, compared to the real stuff, you know, being born and dying. That's where everything happens—in the womb and the grave—the stuff we talk about when we say the word God...it all goes back to this mystery of creation and dissolution...I dunno, I'm rambling again," M said.

There was a pause.

"Are you scared of dying?—Charlotte—I'm curious—"

"No—I mean—it scares me, but now is not my time to be scared—" Charlotte said, "that's the one thing I've learned."

*

M had been officially recognized by the person standing across the street. He swore quietly to himself.

*

Look at Charlotte, he thought: she was *it*, she was the genuine article.

She was too discreet to be touched, to be unshelled: to be consumed.

It was love, he thought, love that took mercy on the soul: that dilated the eyes until they broke under the surface of the skin.

*

M got up to leave, throwing a few dollars on the table, making his apologies swiftly enough to seem sincere.

...because, as a matter of fact, Alice and M were knotted together like two weeds growing through either side of a fence, and because they had simply stopped distinguishing kindness from sex[67] and because Alice knew from the beginning that M was just like her tarot cards had predicted: impossible to love for a million different reasons:

his carrying letters from an English girl he'd never met

his constantly taping new pages into the novel he kept under his bed

his insistence on reading books in languages he barely understood (all of them)

his spending whole nights listening to Jove talk about the constellations

And it was obvious to her that M's infatuations were just ciphers for some deeper image of loss, and that she was just the newest cipher—or anti-cipher—for whatever it was that he had lost.

But she tried anyway—caring for him, letting him into her room, guiding him inside of her like a ship in a storm; it was as easy as taking off a négligée; it was like bundling up wildflowers in an old newspaper and saving them for later—it was an instinct, an instant, a gesture: it was just the way things were between them, or the way they weren't; the way they'd never be.[68]

---

67 Her room was painted pick—she still lived with her parents on the Upper West Side—and it was a small room. An ash colored dress. A gray cigarette lighter. "Play me one of your songs—" "What do you mean—roses are always searching—?" "Come on, just one song—"

68 She waved at M as he walked south along Amsterdam, in a hurry, going in the other direction.

Only Lorca didn't make it to four decades before being put up against a wall and shot; but that was in Spain anyway, and poets could always find other ways to die...

M thought about going back to her apartment, but he didn't.

He imagined the windowpanes were made of paper. He imagined it was a rainy day and that Alice was playing songs on a guitar that was much older than she was.

M thought that Lorca's poems were like *Études* played by a silent man in a speaking world—or like a man looking for his voice in a drop of water.

(Generally, his favorite moment in lovemaking was the moment before he spoke to someone for the first time, looked them in the eye, and sensed their inevitability: then he could hear the *Fado* that was always being broadcast from some distant, metaphysical place.)

While he was on the subway, having fled from Alice for reasons he didn't fully understand, he wrote a poem that might have been a letter to her at the same time:

What determines where you are? The slenderness closed round your head? The sound of roses, singing at your fingers? Who dresses you, then, who takes your clothes and lays them on the bed? And who marks you as one of the dead? (This is what interposes itself between you and a few loose stones at the bottom of a stream: this thinking, this feeling that everything is nominal, like a drop of color unable to escape an enclosure of oil.) The wings of birds are thin. They are like non-dimensional planes: the air cannot slip through them and I cannot describe their resistance except in ethical terms. You are right to have remained where you are. (We are both right, in our own way.)

Alice liked to make love in the middle of the night, in between stages of rapid eye movement dreams, on the occasions that they would wake up at the same time, unaware of where they were—and clasp together—and M would have to force his hand over her mouth so that she wouldn't wake up Wallace and Ellebelle, and she would squirm underneath him, pleasure breaking out all over her body, her teeth trying to clamp down on the palm of his hand.

Happiness, M felt, was about finding a pinhole in the soul of another person so that you could have some visual proof that loneliness was as much of a lie as togetherness—

And it wasn't Alice's fault that she loved him too much; it was his own overdetermined restlessness—

Alice was always so quiet in the shower, and he loved to watch her lather herself—spreading the soap evenly across her face and neck and stomach, across her arms and down along her legs. Her skin was white, almost clear, and the ivory lather made her look ancient to him, like she was from some chalky underworld—and he was careful not to hog the hot water because he enjoyed watching the lather slip away from her body so that suddenly she was human again.

Her skin was the smoothest he had ever felt—when she was clean he liked to lean in and kiss her on the neck—wrap himself around her again.

Later, he would call this the best love[69] he ever had, because it was so silent and so desperate, and because they would fuck until they were both too tired to even recite the days of the week, and because Alice always unbloomed for him right as the moon brightened in the sky, her teeth clenched, her lips pulled back into a wonderful grimace.

And he still thought of La Rondine and everything she had meant to him, so that Alice became a way of refuting the possibility of La Rondine's existence—of turning his old lover into a dream by means of a new, silent and austere love.

And he thought of Lena too—how his seeing Alice was an unforgivable betrayal.

He thought of a lot of things—

69 One of M's favorite passages in all of Calendula: "We must not love because we are bound by laws, either those that we have made or that have been made for us, but out of an inner attunement to the need for the Other…love is always a fulfilling, and a completing, but it is first a detecting. To be attuned to an(other) is to be in harmony with that Other; it is to perceive the pitch of their being and to pitch one's own being in proportion to them. If we are properly attuned to love, our being will constantly be singing and we will constantly be giving love and receiving it. To be a lover is the same as understanding a Bach concerto: it is to understand the grace and beauty of nature. In love, we are like bats pitching our voices against the walls of a dark cave: those who are attuned to love, may navigate the cave, those who are not, fly into the rocky walls, again and again."

La Rondine told me that I should watch *The General* by Buster Keaton, *Stardust Memories* by Woody Allen, and *Death in Venice* by Visconti, and it was a long time before I had the guts to watch those movies and see what she was trying to say to me.

You see, everything tends to come in threes with La Rondine and I: Paris, New York, Milan (cities); Keaton, Allen, Visconti (filmmakers); Joanna, Lena, Alice (rivals); the eleventh, twelfth, thirteenth (days of Guigno).

And New York functions like a Baudelairian mirror world for the invisible we store up inside of us; lisps of leaves, ripples of rain—Paris like the grief of the forgotten; Paris like a letting-go; Paris put to scorn; Milan still ringing in our ears.

Alice asks me about the papers I keep under my bed—I've already caught her reading my letters from Joanna—and all these paths coincide—Antigone drags a body under the city walls—Hart Crane rolls a pair of dice over Melville's tomb—I meet Lena walking over the Brooklyn Bridge—La Rondine writes to me that we must establish a connection with the unknown through the act of giving something and, paradoxically, through the act of destroying something that we love.

And Jove says that the daemonic is built for eternity—but I think it's built to last only so long as we propagate the illusion of its existence—

And think about the processes which freeze the stars and strip the earth of trees and plants and people: these forces that make the notion of human potency not just laughable, but laughably absurd:

And see how each of us becomes a presence that we mark ourselves by, cruelly replacing a distant and unknowable future, and how the spectacle that everyone continues to live for is the spectacle of self-awareness, and how no one realizes that the appearance of moral order amidst moral chaos is a moral miracle.[70]

70   Wallace froze in terror, almost immediately. "Kant you see...transcendental deductions...the impossibility of reason after Nietzsche...Rorty then...and the physics of existential pragmatism...I...you see?" "I have a hard time," Belmonte began ominously, brushing more ash from his sweater, "seeing the connection between Rorty or Nietzsche and Kant; their two projects are almost hilariously antithetical, assuming as one should, that Rorty is merely repeating Nietzsche word for word..." "Yea, what's this stuff about Rorty, if you've read The Mirror of..." M said, trailing off as Wallace slumped from the futon to the floor in despair. "Mmm, ice-cream!" Ellebelle exclaimed, coming back with Herzen from the hallway. "You see everyone is a guide, and every moron and genius and beauty you meet is a free artist of themselves, leading you up out of the absolution of yourself, a little damned dizzy, but still alive; still harkening into the damned everyday," Jove said.

The torn bits of letters taken up like white birds into the sky; he clutched at what was surely nothing—like light through ice—the letters from Joanna he never went anywhere without. The Fisher King at the top of the deck. Alice standing there, sheepishly, now that she'd done it; Alice standing there like he'd deserved it—and he did. Alice saying something about unhappiness; about what makes people happy; about being alone. Alice asking if he'd like to come up, now that she'd forgiven him— Alice waiting for him to follow her king to f9 up to her room; to strip her clean; to bury her in mourning.

A sprig with its flower; Charlotte still counting the change on the table; the sun beginning to bleed itself white—M, trying to catch the bits of letter in his hands like snowflakes—M only managing to catch enough to reconstruct a single unfinished sentence[71]—both of them waiting—moving over the surface of time like two swells upon the sea—both of them wanting to laugh; both of them wanting to follow the letters into the air.

The history of architecture is the history of the struggle for light, he thinks, looking up at the buildings—worlds scooping arcs: firmaments, lined up in a row—it is the miracle of knowing a person without seeing them; the miracle of seeing someone one doesn't know; it is the miracle of the world existing before we arrive...Joanna in London, connecting earth to moon with needle and thread; Joanna sewing herself up in the invisible—Joanna writing letters like light from vanished stars.

71 *I wanted to write to you M because I couldn't do what I truly wanted to do (share a glance across a room, pass by you in a corridor, &c.) and...how does one do that with words? I don't know. I'm trying. I'm trying...*

see joanna you've built this flying machine that is programmed to self-destruct if it looks down but the whole machine isn't built so that you can fly but so that you can deny that the ground exists or that you have feet or toes or shins it's an elaborate but completely ridiculous system...you're human...you're tremendously and simply human and i'm human enough to notice this and even care about it...and i don't think that you think you're deceiving me no that isn't the deception i'm talking about the deception i'm talking about is self-deception of the most melancholy kind the self-deception of someone who sees too clearly who feels the ground too firmly who is all too aware that she has feet and toes and shins that...you aren't a cartoon with a thought bubble above you as much as emailing all the time might make it easy to feel that way no you're sitting there and you're embodied and real and fragile and human and what you have that i need is that fragile real intelligent humanity which is just empathy and is what all of us need but which you and i...don't you think i don't know that you swallow up your emotional responses to the things i send you? you swallow them up and chew them up up and then flatten it out like rice paper which is what i get rice paper...but i know i know i know because even someone as fastidious as you can't eliminate the humanity in your spit the spit you make to chew up the rice and turn it into paper[72]

72 *(& you have to realize & you do realize that i come back to your letters looking for clues in myself & in you as if we were ciphers for what's underneath the ice we've been skating on is it kafka's frozen sea? the clue yes the ax to break up the ice)*

The landscape of a subway station is like a sonata: but I can't hear it unless I close my eyes and listen to the shuffling of the musicians' feet; the exhaling of their breath—it's like the third *Brandenburg*: sawing, blossoming, humming—motion out of being—the salience of spiritual flux—the subway car arriving like the tide; carrying us under the city in a tunnel shedding light like leaves; carrying us to and from a meaninglessness[73] we both understand and reject...

And suddenly I'm above ground again and Brooklyn[74] is starting to pulsate like a star consuming the last of its young from within, or like a wounded animal slinking off to die alone: its silver belly bloated, its eyes staring up at the moon—at the whole galaxy[75] of Ptolemy—a galaxy which is seemingly constructed to conjure up the power of a semi-sinister artist-god.

And my New York is a city of splendor and terror;—and every few weeks I come to a crisis: a women I love abandons me, La Rondine still does not write, the seasons grow too hot or too cold; it does not rain—or it rains too much.

And I just want to record the minutiae of this happiness: the smell of coffee, a young mother holding the hand of her son on the subway, Joanna's letters, Lena's silence, New York like a

73 The myth of the creative class sells coconut waters, Ipads, lofts with faulty plumbing, Ray-Bands, copies of L'Etranger, and subscriptions to N+1: the myth of the creative class is that one can afford to be anything other than oneself.

74 but then there's...what was it? something about mopping up the moonlight like a wet rag...how people correspond to a map of Manhattan with its streets and tunnels and blind alleys, construction zones, traffic and chaos, charm and indifference to poverty, yes... constantly filled and emptied of *agape*, or the overwhelming feeling that everyone else are the ones who've got all the personality and uniqueness and that we're the ones who need to merge with them right away and...all this yapping is lyrical, you know, but the heart's so dense that language bends around the vacuum in the soul like light around a singularity in space...

75 Everything is liable to split and reveal a new gleaming universe at its core. Everything is infinitely divisible.

Schoenberg quartet growing fainter and fainter...

And I want to stand up for beauty, for belief, for good humor; for craft, experience, insight—I want to emerge from this interval of magical, uncertain fiction with my soul on fire; I want the wind to sweep down Knickerbocker in a hurry.

Earth, sky, water—M had been reading the philosopher Georg Calendula all morning—a small book called *Eleatic Exercises*—

Jove had made more green tea, thank God.

"Don't read too much, or you'll be talking Eleatically all week, which is too damn annoying to deal with—" Jove said, handing M a blue mug.

"I'd rather talk Eleatically than Platonically."

"Don't be an idiot, M."

"What would you do if you saw someone on the subway that you never thought you'd see, and if you let them go, and if you didn't know whether you really saw who you thought you saw—?" M asked.[76]

"I'd go look at a Cézanne for some perspective," Jove said.

Belmonte came back from across the hall with an open bottle of wine.

"It has become a cliché to call the postmodern consciousness fragmented, so let us call it something else: out of tune with the musical essence of human character; with our own capacity to love," Belmonte said. "Art must be able to construct itself out of nothing...out of nothing into a suspension bridge between these two self-posited absolutes..."

M nodded in agreement.

Jove rolled his eyes.

Belmonte took a drink straight from the bottle.

76 A woman with eyes like blue marbles; a woman reading a copy of *The Recognitions*; a woman talking to herself in an English accent.

Alice assumed that M was filled with unsayable things too, but she didn't ask so that he wouldn't ask, which was a bargain that they both considered not only fair, but *just* so.

M was looking for something he wouldn't find, she thought: it was like he was looking over her shoulder into some metaphysicians' paradise which she could only understand by listening to the records that he would play for her.

And what was the point of living without love? Alice thought as she watched M take the stairs down to the subway station. There wasn't any, but then again, it was so hard to really capture the little molecules of feeling that swarmed around in her stomach when she thought of M, or when she received one of his letters, or when she tore up the letters of his other lovers (which she did whenever she had a chance to).

These molecules of feeling always slipped through her fingers: only when she sang did any of it make sense; only then did her emotion become heavy and really sink into her soul, rather than float up out of it (only then did she feel like a real bird rather than the mechanical one M had hatched from the golden egg of his consciousness).

*

Simultaneously, Wallace returned to the apartment in Brooklyn with more Chinese food (he was really hungry) and discovered that Ellebelle had changed into overalls and a yellow sunbonnet and had begun scrubbing the floors.

"Hi—" Wallace said, wavering in the doorway, feeling nervous.

"I'm cleaning the floors," she said, "because they're filthy."

"That's because M never cleans them."

"See—" she said, not acknowledging him with her eyes, "that's precisely the problem—M—of course—M—*fucking* M."

"I get it, I'm fucking sick of him too."

Ellebelle glared:

"Don't blame it on M."

"Whaddya mean?" Wallace asked, his nervousness increasing.

Ellebelle shrugged.

Still standing in the doorway, Wallace took a cigarette out from his shirt pocket, along with an orange lighter, and after lighting the cigarette, inhaled deeply with a half-smile:

"Christ Ellebelle—you're giving me a look—"

"You know Wallace, it's the idea of a living death that scares the living shit out of me, you know?—in this relationship—"

Wallace walked over to Ellebelle and dropped his bright cigarette lighter into the bucket of soapy water next to her and watched as it sunk to the bottom of the chemical pool.

"My inner life has no danger, so you can't possibly love me. I'm not stupid Elle—that's what you're about to tell me—that your inner life is full of danger and mine isn't, and so you're bored, and whatever—"

Ellebelle shrugged again.

Wallace kicked the bucket so hard that it went rolling into the wall, shedding water everywhere, and then he grabbed his foot and opened his mouth as if to scream:

*

Simultaneously in Belmonte's apartment, Belmonte said:

"In the eternal transition between human selves, there is no stopping to see where we are."

"I think I've graduated to the next level of He(art) School," Jove said, scribbling in his notebook. "I can feel it in my lungs and bones."

"In the great afternoon of the world—which is the city— there is only coffee and silence. The flag of freedom flies over chaos. Brooklynites declare themselves literate and a baby is born in Park Slope who one day will be king. Basta."

Belmonte was finally out of gin.

"Purgatory isn't exactly a format of reincarnation, but it is an appreciably different form for the soul to take than salvation. Because it is suspended between heaven and hell, the soul in the middle is constantly on the axis between cynicism and sincerity, optimism and despair...I myself, am in a prismatic state of monotonous becoming, always doubling back upon the point of completion so that who I am is a series of probabilities rather than truths," Belmonte explained. "But beware O proud, you shalt be humbled."

*

All the artist-bohemians that Wallace and Ellebelle brought through the apartment day and night looked at Jove as a part of the furniture: a vaguely compelling person designed to maximize the depth of the other objects in the room. People generally wanted something they could take away and condense into an ideogram on the internet: they wanted a version of you that resembled who they thought a person should be. Jove was more sensible than to give in, but sometimes it was impossible not to, just as a byproduct of being Himself. People wanted a system and if they couldn't find it elsewhere they'd find it in who you were, he was sure of that, at least by now—but Jove was tired of telling people that he was an anti-system: that inwardness could never manifest itself as something unified or even clear.

But let 'em think what they wanna think, Jove thought. *Just let 'em.*

Sophocles' weaving of the shuttle. Philomela's tongue. The compounding of pain. Manhattan seen from the distance of a bus leaving town.

I want to cultivate a garden. Live by myself. Swim in the sea. Drink goat's milk with tea.

The sight of Lena crying was really something.

"You'll never hear from me again M..."

Silence.

I thought of phoning for a taxi that could float me out on the Hudson River.

Love is an apostrophe. Love is a catastrophe.

A bus heading toward an invisible abyss. A bus driving through a wormhole in time. A quivering arrow striking against a bell curve in possible realities; ringing out loud.

An eclogue[77] fashioned out of a dream; Pennsylvania nights humming with cicadas and the after-image of a birdsong— New York seventy miles away: waiting, persisting, persisting in

---

77 [Turns tape recorder back on. Lights cigarette] Q: So do you think that *Three Days in Milan* fails to resist idealizing a certain period in your life? A: Well...it doesn't resist it, no...that's why I'm so reticent to talk about it...because the book is a failure in that sense...but you know, I didn't say I agree with what I imagine she'd say...I think there's something useful about idealization. I think maybe, without the ability to see more than what is in front of us, we'd all kill ourselves...that the absence of a God would drive us into a Camusian despair where we're stepping into taxicabs with drivers we know to be crazy and reckless. We'd be willing to throw life away in other words. Idealizations... they are like little toeholds in the sheer rock face of life...they're essential. For me, that toehold, at least in *Three Days*, is M's love for La Rondine. Q: What were you trying to get across in this book? A: Well, there are many beautiful women in this city, and one is not able to make love to them all...and the feeling of watching potential lovers pass by everyday is quite painful, to me at least...and I think that bittersweet feeling is what I wanted to convey in *Three Days*, if not all my novels. Q: Your book also seems to have an ethos, that is, you have an obsession with the difficulty of two people loving each other honestly and openly. A: Yes, that's right. If someone gets that ethic that from reading *Three Days in Milan*, then I suppose that I've succeeded in what I set out to do. Because that's the most important thing: to love without recourse to fantasy or idealization. To love what is true, which is sometimes ugly, and sometimes stupid, and always frustrating.

its chaotic loveliness, persisting in being a sore thumb in my imagination.

Milky afternoons, late in August. Rain on the tin awning of the house I grew up in.

And then this conscious sense of loss: the loss of something radiant within—OK again—my movements are clumsy—my goodbyes are worse.

All I have with me is my endless novel, an idea for a film, and a thermos filled with black coffee.

I'll come back on a winter day when no one is looking.[78]

78 (And then there are things I still haven't told you...) Well, all these things secure your devotion when you least expect it: friends and their lovers, warm beer and ethics, cheap wine, art history, Pessoa's names, a way through doubt and fear, Shakespeare's clowns, the classical music in the bus terminal, sage tea, sunlight—sex without kissing until the very last second. "Save us from generalizations!" Chekhov cried. "Give me life!" Falstaff cried.

Bunched violets without roots and a stillness that says "no more meaning"—

The black and white photograph of La Rondine I took in the Milan metro—here: I'll pinch it between my thumb; rip it, one...two—scatter it like ash across New York—my unrepaired city; New York—my mirror for loneliness.

My fingers are in her mouth; broken stems—her throat is crying "I can't I can't".

An apple floats down from the top of a tree—my life with her arrives at an enchanted emptiness; paints itself over a void—a life which rests like a feather inside a bowl of water. I want to say: *screw everything that isn't a poem, a film, a photograph*—screw any city where a soul can fall through the air and not fracture its bones.

And again: a stillness that says: no more meaning.

So no more to the Debussy string quartet—no more to moonless nights; no more to letters, images, diaries—no more to anything that isn't a trial; no more to anything that isn't a tango danced to the very, very end—a tango that demands the courage of maniacs and poets; that excludes all the rest; all other kinds of courage. And no more to the random solving and unsolving of philosophical puzzles. No more halting, no more stopping to wet one's finger and test the wind. No more to anything that isn't Kafka's frozen ax wielded against the frozen sea within. No more lies[79] and no more self-deception.

And because I have this instrument—I call it a poem—I can turn lies to incredible truths; because I have this instrument—I'll

79 Another excerpt from Calendula: "A philosophy of love is, in part, a material phenomenology of subjective life; how we are (how we exist) within our bodies. A philosophy of love must not forget that love takes place between human beings and not spirits or angels. Love is corporeal, finite, and contingent. A philosophy of love must instruct us how to embody love; how to love the corporeal, finite, contingent world."

call it a weapon—I'll turn it against myself.

I wrote La Rondine a poem instructing her on how to pass through space and time: *from Milano Centrale to Grand Central Terminal...a tear in space...a hole in the ceiling...like what Rilke wrote "what birds plunge through is not the intimate space"...the distant, blueish void...past interleaved with future...*

And is the process of transformation, I wonder, continuous or discrete or dialectical? Does the present become memory slowly, or all at once?

Does it shed its presentness like an outer layer to reveal the kernel of memory that is always there—*inside?*—waiting—

A year after he last saw her, M figured La Rondine still hated the tango and cherished the anonymity of crowds.

I've thought of you a million times, he wrote to her in a letter he never sent, *but I can't let the inequity of eros scale itself down into something manageable.*

It was inexplicable the way that the flesh got laughed at, or how the airless flower of a person veiled itself in awkwardness.

The older he got, the more M realized that people caused each other to suffer because they couldn't imagine any other way to be: mouths filled with blood: lungs ripped up like old letters in the wind.

This is my wounded humanism: that dying in the last swell of winter, I do not repent of you, or your sex.

This is the unrecovered discontent: the feathers and dust that clutter the floor like scraps.

Only people with jaws like pike fish can bite through the silence they have tried to swallow. Only lovers who are guilty of physical unselfing can claim they are not deceived, La Rondine.

Stay with me, bait me into a new exercise.

(Only the parallel net is thrown over you, as with me; dragging us in by the throat.)

Japanese silks and Chinese vases: that was the fragile wonder of the soul: the soul and the dance. Ellebelle swaggering in the kitchen making coffee. Alice's white ass naked on the futon; her slim green eyes. Cimetière Marin; Van Gogh yellows; Lena dancing on the roof as within a budding grove. All this imagery producing cause-and-effect. All this imagery producing nameless girls and summer dresses; figures hidden behind screens; Lena painting herself out of a corner; Lena painting herself into my novel. Alice being jealous of what she doesn't understand. Lena and La Rondine. La Rondine and Joanna. (A nonsense game I make up to pass the time.) Washington Square as the sun goes down. The light years I'm keeping close by. The light years I don't let go of. (Years as violet, and as violent, as the rain.)[80]

80 The blue moon quivers and sheds its petals of violet-blue (as blue violets float) in the cold basin of the bluemoon in the cold rippling water of the blue moonlight rippling in the hollows of the bluemoon petal rippling and shedding the fragment shells of the cold blue moonlight (and the cinders of the trees quivered in blue).

She noticed every strand of color floating in the crowd, scarves and hats, dresses, and suitcases, each scrap pinwheeling around her, merging in the periphery of her vision, slipping in and out of sight.

Love, her grandmother used to say, is what it means to taste color and to drink sunlight.

And where was M now?—M who had been trying to find her his whole life and who would look for her after she was gone.

The whole terminal of Milano Centrale was glowing with anticipation; a feeling was rippling out from her core, like a butterfly that had burst out of its wrappings, or the last note of a Bach partita, trembling on a violin string—

It was love, she thought, it was love that was the most impossible, and perfect, and necessary thing in the world—

It was exquisite: this strange, charged anticipation in her body: her whole life quivering out ahead of her, as if the future were a series of moments (like butterflies to be captured, second by second, and pinned by the wing to her breast)...

She wanted to gather her perceptions together, so delicate and bright, and bundle them like a bunch of flowers in her hand...

The tragic[81] was embedded in life; she could feel that too: surging alongside this current of love.

81 We are so desperate for love that we don't kiss, and prefer to hold each other in the silence of the train station, and space and light bend across the vectors of the main terminal and become stuck like glue in your hair, and your hands, and your teeth... I've always believed this was possible, this strange, obliterating silence and it's ours now, our responsibility, and maybe that's why you're trembling, and why you're speaking so fast in your bad English, crying O Dio mio (whenever you make a mistake, which is often) and my God, you are so deeply moving to me, speaking this language that birds speak: Plato's bastard Greek, and Shakespeare's too: always shedding forms; whispering love, then despair, then terror; always changing, always wavering 'like a moon on water' you whispered to me that night in Paris: and when you said it, you shook.

And it was you all along my little fox with your brown eyes and your brown hair falling over your eyes like a romantic poet and your seriousness which you mix so suddenly with laughter blooming from your lips like an alpine flower in the snow but you really are so stupid sometimes for a fox you don't know what I'm feeling at all whole worlds that burst and break apart and fuse again and can't you read them in the stars? before you notice that I'm crying telling you I can't forget the lion Alessandro because I loved you both I have so much love inside of me it would kill me to make love to you both as long as I'm with him but it's you I want little fox I just don't have the courage left I'm not free I'm scared of the rupture but o mio dio it's time it's time I let myself go to a man let me have him and use me not like the lion uses me with his body but with his soul and we could get a little place in Paris and go for morning walks along the Seine and you could do your writing and I wouldn't bother you maybe I'd have affairs but you wouldn't mind because you'd have affairs too it'd be like we were walking backwards through life and wouldn't that be perfect that mixed up broken kind of life that never falls into place but never falls out of it either and we'd use each other but it would be so perfect that we wouldn't mind please don't forget that this kind of love never leaves a person that it turns us to salt or ash before it lets us go and the night I heard you play the piano upstairs in the Shakespeare and Company I cried because you were so beautiful and you didn't even notice me sitting there listening and it was a miracle when I saw you again writing by the Notre Dame and now I swear you're my connection to poetry and love and I know you must be writing about me somewhere and that you can't forget either and maybe this is what it's like to be dead just a stream of memories and feelings rippling out into the universe like radio waves growing weaker and weaker the further out they get but still going on

and on my love for you which I'm sure is something that we
made up together love but decided to believe in anyway when
you said to me that last night in Milan that you loved me it was
so soon but I was such a coward then what difference does it
make if we've known each other for five minutes for five years if
there's love there's love you don't need to lie about it like there's
some independent standard it's only what we feel but you aren't
perfect either you are always falling in love and I know that
I'm not the only one because you poets think your metaphysical
rivers will carry you wherever you like but there are limits if
you think about how if someone is so special you can't just make
love to anyone how if you love a woman if you write a poem
about her if you learn how to see the world through her eyes you
can't just fall in love with somebody else and I wouldn't make
love to you and maybe that's why you won't give yourself to me
completely and why I didn't meet you in Berlin and why we can't
run off together or why we can't live up to the stories we told
each other because we're real and because we aren't characters in
a book and and because real people are broken and a little magic
and poetry can't fix them and because you think you know what
love means but you men don't know anything you really don't I
swear it's the only thing I know for certain and yes I also believe
we are meant to love and that the poets always knew it and Plato
knew it *love* that love gives us access to the divine which is why
you are here my little fox (in my thoughts) and why you're gone
so soon because you just wanted to get a glimpse of the higher
life and remember how you were so crushed the first night I said
I couldn't stay with you in Milano that my mother said I had
to come home you know I've never seen anyone so sad and you
were so weak sitting there on the metro steps like you couldn't
move like I was water rushing over you eroding your will and we
started growing old right then and there and it'll keep getting
worse we'll stop pretending we'll see each other again because

you can't love anyone you need as much as you need me and I'll
have to remain separate from you or I'll just die I'll become a
woman like my sister who teaches school children so meek and
careful around her husband her whole self withered like a rose
in winter and I think that getting old means letting time move
faster and not resisting it so much just floating through it like
you float on a sea of jello and do you remember eating Indian
food with me and meeting my friends who spoke the worst
English you'd ever heard and how I didn't put sugar in my coffee
(just) for you because you told me how bad it was for me and
that you never used sugar because you don't eat anything good
except for fruit and leaves like an animal (so pure) or maybe you
are just afraid of the body decaying and dying forever but you
know there's no fountain of youth there's just love that grabs you
by the hair and lifts you up to the sky so your toes curl and you
gasp and wail the wished for words and I'll go back to the Lion
after you're gone (from my thoughts) and what choice do I have?
because you just want to keep me as an image for your book and
because I can't wait for ever because you could live with just my
memory but I need real love and you have so many needs but
they all exist in the air for you my little fox like poems these
memories our memories and I think we've created the perfect
image and I'll watch it break apart and do you remember it?
those few hours kissing in the Jardin des Plantes and midnight
in that little hotel room in Milan and a few last kisses before the
train you had to take was leaving the rain streaming through my
hair and how tired we were from being unable to consummate
what we knew was true that it would have been too much that
I'd have been broken because that's what love does for the first
time in your life if you need someone and know they'll be gone
like I knew you would: *it breaks you.*

M noticed a young girl in a pink dress running around the fountain in Washington Square, her golden hair flush with light.[82]

He put down his book.

"So underneath the surface of the poem there's only another surface..." he said to himself.

When La Rondine rose in the morning, M suddenly imagined, she spread her clothing for the day underneath a window in the Italian sunlight and her breasts swayed like full-blown roses.

"Reelka? Reelka?" someone was saying to M...who was

82 And you can always tell the broken-hearted ones by the way their eyes look lost in a crowd, searching for someone they know they will never see again, and I have always counted myself among the people of this scattered tribe, which is why I can recognize it so easily in others. But all this, this book, these koans—I'm writing this only so that I can find you; so that you will recognize me in a crowd one day; so that my eyes will always be searching for your eyes in the crowd, the eyes that I know have been sent to look for me too. And La Rondine, I think we will find each other again when we're old and you'll have raised a family in Milan, and become fat and sentimental, and that will be it for us—like the end of a little ballad plunked out on a stand up piano, wavering like a woman's voice, or a moon on water—and we'll kiss and maybe you'll feel like we did when we watched the swallows dip through space and time; when you were young and you kissed me with a fire that made my toes curl and my lips tremble...and I'll never forget the rain that last morning, the rain like the death in everything—the death that's everywhere in the novel I'm writing to remember you and to keep you alive...the novel which has become about me and my lovers and my friends, more than you—if only because the shimmering intensity of the everyday flows through me like the sunlight flows through the glass of water on my kitchen table...and it is you, La Rondine, who are the newest refutation of time—this is your secret: that you do not exist like the rest of us do, that you have found a way into the dreams of others, that you have found a way to mix the ashes of death in with the violets of memory, and a way to mix mustard seed in with the coming of the spring. And watch: moonlight changes all the way down in the air, like music as it rises out of the water, and though isn't quite summer yet, you can feel how warm the air is, and you can see how the trees are full and yellow; how the pink buds are half open in the night; how they curl back over themselves like old hands finding each other across a hospital bed. And what a romantic fool I am, writing to you—the woman I've lost and will always lose—at the edge of the fountain...writing to you until you appear out of nowhere...like a swallow (thus my name for you Gloria): falling through a shadow in time.

so busy thinking that he didn't see a very tall old man[83] with a handlebar mustache standing in front of him.

"Reelka. You are reading Reelka, no? Young man?"

M nodded.

"Of course, the world is unintelligible to the young...only the old, you realize...how we see it. How very darkly these... tease tsings...they...how beautiful they are, yes. Like Reelka..."

M nodded again.

A world forgotten by angels. A memory of a forgotten world.

M watched the golden-haired girl splash through the fountain.

83 Georg Calendula

I locate desire where your spine bends and your navel flattens, rippling like a chord of light. And whatever you are, you are, Dancer, strange one, with your head full of secrets and songs like rain. City girl, stranger: always one step out of time...you are lovely and bohemian in the way that you shuck across the park: your eyes rolled back, your hands on your breasts. And only out of indifference would I have loved you. (Lavender crocuses and Roman hyacinths...) New York: my radiant unknown. City girl: my radiant known...the spring night is a membrane through which I receive you into my existence...and I am too unsymmetrical, too rough for the beautiful which forms like a skin over the moonlight; the beautiful which you tie around your waist like a loose sash as you stand, swaying, at the window. And I ask you to reach down into the tangle of my nerves: to bundle my consciousness of love into a paper-rose. (And who are you?)

Lena takes a bath in the springtime, and keeps the windows closed so the glass gets cloudy, and occasionally with her mouth she makes a "plop" sound to pass the time, and in the other room she has put on a record of Beethoven's final[84] quartet, the *16th*, and maybe later she'll put on Schubert's *Quintet in C* ... and she is crying very quietly, listening to the music, her tears only interrupted by the "plop" sound she makes with her lips, or the occasional "hwish" of the water rippling when she circulates her arms to keep warm.

Next to the tub she has a book open with a single phrase underlined in blue—*"like the tender fires of stars moments of their life together"*—and there are watermarks all over the underlined page, from writing in the tub, or crying, or both.

She knows, in her own irrational way, that she only lives in the mind of some writer—and for this reason she writes him long love letters that she never sends because she knows he's already read them—because she is a part of him, and because he loves her already and because she is terrified that he'll forget her—and because poets always forget the women they love.

And this is why she's listening to such sad music: because she knows that his love isn't real, that it's just the refraction of his desire for some other woman.

When it begins to rain outside, she laughs to herself, and slides down in the tub so that she is almost completely submerged and waits for the sound of the rain to merge with the texture of the quartet.

When the record ends, she leaps out of the tub—dripping bathwater all over the linoleum floor.

She turns the record from side one to side two.

84 "To love like this is to reach the absolute depth of love, for God does not love us because we are perfect, but because he will one day perfect us in heaven. And to love in the way that Beethoven composed his last quartets, is to love with this incredible divine tenderness the imperfect, the aging, the dying: the entirely mortal."

I watch a ripple of water spread from the edge of the center of the fountain—La Rondine, I blame myself for losing you in the fractured reality of water; I'm close to broke—and I've filled too many notebooks with memories of your gestures and ways of speech.

(The transformation of everydayness: every drop of color into the creation of meaning.)

Lena and I mimic lovers who are genuinely angry with each other, in short—we've become mannerists. But this book began with the hope of writing to you, for you, about you; completely unsentimentally—with the hope of being gentle with my old attachments—but how difficult that becomes when the intoxication of the absolute sets in: when the old men playing chess begin to resemble Rodin's thinkers, and young girls in the fountain resemble the redemption of a Botticelli angel.

You know that scene in *8 ½* where Mastroianni and Claudia Cardinale go for a drive in the middle of the night?—the scene where Mastroianni realizes that he can't *really* love Claudia, that he can only idealize her?—Fellini put that scene in just so that he could show what resolution really means in art (as in life): letting our symbols stand in for what they really are—*symbols.*

The beauty of wordshed, of language going limp with exhaustion, pleasure, and despair.

Fathomless memories.

Knee-deep in lilies.

And what if we framed our lives as a way of giving love?—and said that nothing—that not even our grief—was worth perishing for except for It—the giving of love?

What if we said all that and did not believe it?—[85]

85 ...like we were the black prince, trying to outfox a kingdom of lies.

96

We can answer as did the Greek, who upon hearing the argument of Zeno of Elea that "movement is an illusion" (since an arrow in flight remains motionless) got up and walked out of the amphitheater.

The twentieth century gives us a simple touchstone for reality: physical pain...and it is a joy taking a future we don't understand and spinning it like silk between our fingers; pushing consciousness through a few tunnels in time, emerging in Paris or New York or Milan again and again, in a loop, carrying past versions of ourselves back and forth like jars of water across a desert, hoping, for our own sakes, that we stumble, and let the jars break and release their contents into the sand.

And there are puzzles too, puzzles we have already laid out and rearranged: the fragments of a few days two summers apart, the letters I wrote to Lena from Pennsylvania, the letters I wrote every morning to Joanna in London that I never sent, or only sometimes—

And inside of a brain, desire finds itself in control of a few marionette limbs that produce little quivers of uncertainty and permissive pleasure—but what does this mean?—because under the backdrop of New York City, I can see everything anew— how many precious lies we told—how unprepared I was for the magical weaving of nights into a life of realistic happiness; how when I took the bus [86] from Port Authority, I wasn't just leaving

---

86 "Don't you think that...it's terrible how we waste each other...how every time we see each other we end up just looking at each other with looks of wonder and pain? I mean... Christ Lena. Do you know how wonderful it is that we even met?—in this whole black terrifying universe—that two people could understand each other a little bit...God—it was so long ago now...not in real terms, not that long ago...but...it feels like it...it feels like we've become different people; like we're responsible for carrying on the commands given to us by our past, idiotic selves—" "Yes, that's it...we were two idiots, but the difference is—I don't think we've changed." "Maybe not—no." "You have no idea how much I love you M..." M kissed Lena on the neck. "It's like being a child again...lovers are always like children, the way they act..." "You poor fool M."

Lena and Wallace and Ellebelle and Belmonte and Jove—I was leaving the whole world of enchantment and magic and deception behind.

Black acacias. Weeping willows. A garden gate. A nap in the sun.

This is a responsive, emotional peace: this isn't anything other than the demand of the will to be disposed. Human, anti-human...

La Rondine said Paris was like water; she dangled her feet over the banks of La Seine and said that she wanted to know me: *that she wanted to know who I was.*

"I want to wipe away the moonlight that has muddied everything up for us Lena…I want to wipe away the sadness of you…to live alone with a woman who can understand me… to pass away my life in the recognition of what is always dying within us…the flowers of love, the hairs that stood up on your arm when I used to touch you…you know?—some mornings I wake up without despair for you or anyone else…I dunno—I wish I didn't—it's a fucked up thing, not to miss anyone—"

"Do you remember how it was to be together and to be alone and to think of nobody but each other? How we would read *Mrs. Dalloway* out loud together, and cry…and be so unbelievably happy M?"

"I feel like this isn't *it*—you know—that it will rain later and that we'll put on a movie—something that reminds me of you something by Almodovar, *Hable Con Ella* or *Abrazos Rotos*…but *this is it,* Lena…I can't say much more; it just has to be. I don't know why. I know why, but I don't. I know I have to go—"

"Do you remember that time we ran into each other at that bar in Williamsburg?—how you asked to see me out the door, and how you started kissing me on the street and then how we jumped into a cab together? That haunted me for days, like you were asserting your possession over me…and since then?—it's like you don't even have to be around, physically…it's horrible, I mean—I should hate you M—but mostly, I pity you—"

"We were in love Lena—or something—we were *something*—how can you blame me for doing that?—"

"All this introspection is just a way of exonerating yourself from all this shit…you know?—you're just as much a part of it M—human fallibility and weakness—you're as much a part of it as everyone else—and you just don't want to admit it—"

"You know who has the toughest job in the world?" M asked, after a long pause.

"Who?"

"Metaphysicians[87]—because their research is always inconclusive and pointless...and because it hurts to have to think about life and death every waking second...and that's what it feels like trying to talk to you Lena; or being intimate with you...it's like doing metaphysics—and I'm tired of it Lena—"

"Uh-huh."

"I'm gonna go, I think—" M said, making a face with his bottom lip that resembled regret, "my bus is here—"

"Cya M."

"Cya."

"Arrivederci."

"Ciao."[88]

---

87 "We can imagine that when the philosopher of love sits besides us at a piano, he does not create new scales for us to play, he does not rewrite Mozart or Schubert to make them easier to play, rather, that the philosopher of love patiently listens to us stumble over the scales, stumble over the accidentals and octaves in the great works, gently explaining to us where we have gone wrong, how the piece must sound, the rightest ring of it: the truest tempo."

88 The earth is still moist and pliant and the air is less humid, after the rain. She watches the bees dazzle on the tops of flowers and she thinks to herself that she has been stripped of death completely; that she is as white and slender and empty as she feels on the inside now, on the outside, with her toes in the grass and the night still aching on the back of her tongue...she cries out and sinks to her knees in the wet grass and rolls on her back sobbing with a strange happiness. Already, she can feel her imagination straining towards the crush of the evening, the glittering summer darkness; the deepening of the already lovely day—and yes, she can feel it in her breast: love, more real than anything—a love, like some unbelievable whitewash of stars burning overheard...she realizes, with a slight smile, that this is somebody's dream—and that, as surely as some other being lives and breathes and dies in her, she lives and breathes and dies in someone else; and that if they exist only through each other—her imagined companion and herself—through their love for one another—and she knows that if one of them falls out of love, then there will be an end; and they will become, suddenly, just as they were before they loved each other: a gorgeous nothing.

We said it was by faith that we ascended. And we said that when the adagio started (like it's starting now) that we would be prepared. And we were here, we were waiting, already ruined by the music, already ruined by the sense of time that we said the music itself enclosed. And you said it was like a great thirst, you said it was an unknowing suddenly come upon the soul: a desire as empty as a cloud in heaven. And La Rondine, we were always thinking of music when we thought of ourselves, we were always thinking of how the heart imagines a mystery breathing inside a rose.

We wanted to restore ourselves to the nature that we agreed was like a hand, opening a window in the spring. And we wanted that nature to be single within us: we wanted it to grow from a single root, deep inside the ground. We wanted an adagio as brief as a mourning: we wanted the music to disguise itself in our letters, our absence, our distance. We wanted the stars to swarm thick as gnats: we wanted to see the same stars that fell through the cracks of Castello Sforzesco the night before I left. And we wanted our dispossession to return to us, finally, La Rondine, as something familiar: *as breathing*.

And dispossession could become our faith La Rondine, and in a way, it already has, because we are as loveless as the cities we moved through and searched across: we are as loveless as two waves, running, one after the other, into annihilation on a shore of light.

springlight my love our mudbodies ruffled in black heaps
all musical together like disarrays of falling stars your mouth my
mouth our eyes sewn together crushed deep together the bowl
of figs on the table eat one come on sunlight dappling spreading
over the floor this surplus of life we break into eating with our
hands our fill kiss me again and look! the little sunflower pods
we grew in the glass jar are shooting up all green around us (like
generations of people springing up from the earth) and it's so
wonderful the way we live and die and the way that you say that
"here is meaning" and "kiss me again" and remember the stars
when the world was at creation? and how the sparrows were flying
through crannies in walls of Milano Centrale (burnished all gold
as the sun was setting) and you were exactly as I remember you
(the bowl of figs was so sweet so tough) and the grief of losing
I suppose was tough enough to make us faithless (it was grief
enough to make us faithless again) and faithless forever my love
(faithless so that we'll be faithful forever) faithless so that we'll
be faithful for good

N

"*It was in Milano Centrale that he last saw La Rondine, and it was in Grand Central Station that he knew, somehow, he would see her again. The two terminals were linked (in the way that the dreams of strangers may be linked) by the metaphysical rivers of time, which, as they flowed delicately across the plains of memory, gathered the sediment of existence into the single manifold of the sea...which was death, and which he sometimes called love.*"

-M, *Three Days in Milan*

ow tell me you'd like to parachute just for the feeling of clutched-silk against your ribs—this is what Joanna wrote back when I told her about La Rondine.

But I'm afraid of heights (and of flying too)—so instead, I took a piece of chalk and drew a moon on water.

fin

Acknowledgements:

Dear thanks goes to Alex Traube, Daniel Bossert, Kelly Swope, Daniel Vallejo, and of course, my sister and my parents.